THE OPPOSITE OF MEMORY

A COLLECTION OF UNFORGETTABLE FICTION

MARY E. LOWD

CONTENTS

For my grandparents—
Elsie who I barely knew, Wes who wrote books for her; Bill who
picked out a car for me, and Pearl who became a core part of my
family in her final years

PREFACE

My grandmother was diagnosed with early onset Alzheimer's when I was nine. She died two years later. I'm told that once Grandma Elsie was diagnosed, those who knew her realized there had been signs of her mental decline going back at least a decade. So, I remember Grandma Elsie, but I never really knew her. I didn't get the chance. But that's the realization of a woman in her early forties, looking backward. At the time, I was nine, and we didn't know if her Alzheimer's was the genetic kind. We didn't know if my dad—who had always been famously forgetful—would begin to disappear into his own mind in the coming decades. We didn't know if Alzheimer's was the way that I would—one day, eventually—also die. It's a brutal way to die. You forget the people you love. They become strangers around you, while you search for them, not recognizing who they've become, only knowing them as what you remember, and not understanding why these strangers lie and claim to be people they're clearly not. Grandma Elsie never stopped looking for her red-headed soldier husband; she couldn't see him in the grey-haired old man who kept appearing in their house. Eventually, your mind decays to the point where you forget how to eat. You starve to death, unable to understand what's happening to you or why.

Maybe Alzheimer's can be handled more humanely, but this is what I watched happen to my grandmother when I was between the ages of nine and eleven. My grandfather wrote a book about his experiences caring for her—My Wife Has Alzheimer's by J. Wesley Sullivan. It's an important book, and I've made sure to keep it in print, so his voice can provide company to anyone else undergoing a similarly horrifying, impossibly lonely ordeal. He made mistakes in his choices, I think, but it was an untenable situation. Even handled perfectly, it would have been brutal.

And all the while, as my mom went every week to care for Grandma Elsie, giving Grandpa Wes needed respite, I wondered: will this some day happen to me? Will I some day tear paper into tiny strips all day, because my mind is so far gone that the soothing sound of the tearing paper is all that's left to me?

That's a heavy burden for anyone to bear, let alone a ten-year-old child.

I spent a lot of time thinking about memory—what it means, how it matters, and what happens when it fails. And I learned, partly from watching my grandfather, that part of how you process horrible things that happen to you is: you write books about them.

My grandfather was a newspaper man; my uncle writes hiking books. I had writers as examples in my family. Also, my mother—who is profoundly generous and kind—loves literature to an extreme degree. So, it's not really that surprising that I became a writer. And it's even less surprising, really, that my fiction returns again and again to questions of memory. The first story I ever sold, "Forget Me Not," is about a man addicted to a memory drug. I revisited that same memory drug in the story, "A Second Enchanted Evening," and then fifteen years later, I returned to the characters from "Forget Me Not" with a sequel story, "The Fish Kite."

Not every story in this book is directly about memory. Some of them are about knowledge and identity. The intersection between memory, technology, identity, and reality. Because those things are all intimately intertwined. And all together, they add up to who we are.

I took the thing that scared me most—losing my memories—and I built little boxes where I could break such a big concept down into smaller pieces, package them up, examine them from every angle, and then store them safely... each piece inside a story, and each story inside a book. This book is about trauma, self-discovery, and reinvention. We don't have to let our fears rule us. Instead, we can own them and incorporate them into recreating ourselves as who we want to be.

NOTE ON THE 2ND EDITION

This book was originally released in 2014 before I had really finished writing it. My first two novels—*Otters In Space* and *Otters In Space 2: Jupiter, Deadly*—had recently been picked up by a small publisher, FurPlanet, and I wanted to sell copies at local events. However, a table with only two books on it is a sad affair. So, I took all the short stories I'd written at the time and managed to put together three meagre collections—*Welcome to Wespirtech*, *Beyond Wespirtech*, and *The Opposite of Memory*—which I self-published. For the next nine years, I pursued traditional publishing, and my self-published collections fell to the side. But now that I'm in my forties and tired of the nonsense inherent to the publishing industry, I've returned to my roots, and it was time to make this book what it was always meant to be.

More than half of the stories in this book were written after the first edition was released, and two of them are brand-new, never published before. I never stopped loving this book, even when it was incomplete. Now that I see what it's become, I love it even more. I hope, dear reader, you will love it too.

1

FORGET ME NOT

His confidence drew her to him. The gleam in his eye said "I can take on the world," and she believed it. Here was a man who could not fail. She was fascinated, and her fascination endeared her to him.

Michael introduced them, but neither Joan nor Leland bestowed a second glance on Michael all night. Their eyes and conversation were reserved for each other.

Five months later, Joan and Leland were living together in a penthouse apartment downtown with a view of Mount Hood, functioning smoothly as a couple. Michael came over for dinner every second or third night. Their home was his second home, and he was best friend and confidant to each of them. Proud of his role, he boasted loudly of having introduced them. He couldn't find a girl of his own, he'd say, but he sure could find them for his friends, couldn't he? Leland would concur, but Joan would just smile and get Michael a second drink.

"When are you doing the parents thing?" Michael asked one night. "I know you're thinking of getting married..."

"So, we better hurry up and get our parents involved? Or else they won't pay for the wedding?" Leland joked.

"That'd be a shame," Michael said. "With our company topping the market, you couldn't possibly pay for a wedding yourself."

Leland grinned. "We're only up there, kid, because I have such a competent engineer."

Michael bowed his head to the compliment, and the men clinked glasses. Though, they all knew it wasn't Michael's engineering that carried *Doohan Gadgetry* to the top. Perhaps it kept them there, but Leland's uncompromising entrepreneurship was the instrumental ingredient.

"Actually," Joan said, "we already have done the parent thing."

"That's great. How'd it go?"

"Well, Joan's parents loved me."

"Who wouldn't?"

"I mean it. Her dad and I really hit it off, and her mom's got the best, driest sense of humor I've ever heard. Better than yours, Michael."

They both turned to Joan. She hesitated but said only, "Leland's mother was very nice."

"It's just my mom," Leland added, "Dad died when I was a little guy."

"I remember," Michael said. "Was your brother there?"

Leland laughed right out loud. "What a guy! Michael, I don't know what I'd do without you."

The interchange stayed at that, until Leland retired to his home office for the night. He had work to catch up on, a meeting to prepare for in the morning, plenty to keep him busy. Joan saw him to his book lined cell, kissed him on the cheek, and closed the solid oak door behind him. As she did, she heard him muttering, and she thought she caught the word "brother."

"What was that about?" she asked Michael, back in the living room. "Does Leland have a brother?"

"He likes to deny it. I think they're mad at each other. I met him a long time ago... Before Leland's first company crashed. I was an engineer for him back then too."

"Leland had a company crash?"

"He doesn't like to talk about that either. He doesn't like to talk about failing."

"He gives off the impression of a man who couldn't fail... Or, at least, a man who never has." Joan sipped her drink. "You'd think it'd scar him."

"Well, that's probably why he doesn't talk about it. He's keeping it out of his mind."

Joan and Michael chatted on, finishing their drinks. Come two o'clock that morning, Joan finally saw him to the door. She grew quiet, and leaned against the doorframe in such a way that Michael could see something was wrong.

"What is it?" he asked.

"Leland's mother didn't say anything when Leland talked about growing up alone... How hard it was, just the two of them, after his dad died." Joan played her fingers along the doorframe. Then she stopped and looked Michael square in the face: "Did you ever meet Leland's mother?"

He shook his head.

"She looked sad. But it was a cheerful sad... The kind that hides its tears."

Michael touched Joan's cheek and wished her goodnight. He was right, though he did not say it: a mother would be sad when her sons did not speak. But, Joan wondered if that was all. Why did she play along? If she were Leland's mother, she'd be angry at her sons' childishness. She wouldn't pretend to have one son at a time, even if her sons pretended not to have brothers.

∾

Joan kept hoping to talk with Michael about Leland's past again, but she never got the chance. One week later, Michael was hit by a car crossing Burnside near Powell's Books. Leland was there, browsing the new window displays. He looked up from a magazine about the latest Fortune 500s to see a ratty old Jaguar plow into Michael.

He couldn't have done a thing. Yet, Leland blamed himself, and Joan got to see what happens when the man who can't fail finally does. He breaks.

The daring, fearless, entrepreneurial spirit that carried Leland and his company to the top abandoned him. He claimed that *Doohan Gadgetry* couldn't get by without Michael, but in truth, there were plenty more engineers. It was the fearless lion who once was Leland that his company couldn't get by without. He questioned his choices, lent credence to his second thoughts and crippled himself with self-doubting indecision.

Joan cried too, and found solace in their shared grief at night. But she was seeing only the half of it: At work, she still functioned, crying only at home. She felt like a hollow shell, but it was just that: *A feeling*. She carried on.

True understanding waited until she came home one night and found Leland sprawled on the floor, leaning against the couch: He was gripping an orange plastic medicine bottle.

"I have to make it go away," he said. He looked like a man bitterly drunk, but he was only drunk on tears.

"What have you taken?" Panic tinged her voice. Joan took the bottle and read the label.

"I haven't taken it yet... I was waiting for you."

～

On her second date with Leland, Joan had asked him, "What was your childhood like?"

"Good. Happy," he laughed.

"Tell me a story from it."

"Okay," he said. "I entered a kite contest once. I spent a week designing and building a kite shaped like a fish. A giant, silvery, scaled fish, flying in the sky. The scales had to be cut out and glued on individually. I remember getting a cramp in my neck, hunched over my work table for hours. I had to get it just right."

"Did you win?"

"I don't remember." He laughed again. "It was beautiful though. On the test run, it positively sparkled... looked like it was swimming in the sky. I'll have to show you sometime. If I can ever find it..."

Joan had smiled at the time, but now the memory took on an ominous tone.

A lot of Leland's childhood had seemed hazy, but Joan's memories from that age weren't so good either. When they got to talking about Leland's career, the stories were of one success after another. Up and up and up. Leland lived in a can-do world, and Joan had loved being swept up into it.

But now she had to face the price.

~

"You *have taken it*," she said. "You took it after your company crashed, and after you fought with your brother... When else? How many times?"

"I can't remember."

"Of course not." There was bitterness in her voice.

"I mean, I can't remember the number. Every time. I take it every time."

"So you do have a brother?"

"Yes."

"Do you *remember* him?"

"I remember. I remember! I remember. And I want to forget.

The pain reminds me. Brings it all back. And now Michael dying... I can't take that. I can't suffer through this one with you. If I do, it will bring them *all* back. All the memories. I'm just starting to taste them again. On the fringes of my mind. My life is riddled with them."

"All our lives are."

"Not like mine. Not like mine. My dad... my senior prom... getting kicked out of Catlin Gable... all the money trouble..." Leland flipped through memories seemingly too painful for him to recount. He latched onto an easier one: "That kite contest... when I was a kid? I *lost* that contest. I dropped my fish-kite in the mud and everyone trampled it. It was *ruined*, and that's why I can't find it. I lost, and it was my own fault too. Clumsiness. I can't remember things like that. I can't *afford* to remember things like that. How would I go on?"

"We all go on. We all fail, and we all go on." She paused, "We'll go on together."

"No." He shook his head. "No, no. But you can take it too. We'll forget together. It'll all be the same as before."

"Except without Michael."

"That can't be helped now."

Joan looked at the label on the bottle: "*Amnesia Inducing. For medicinal uses only. Keep away from children and those with memory disorders.*"

How could she comfort him? He was feeling the pain of every failure, every loss, every bad moment since early childhood. Scrapes and cuts that should have been kissed better years ago bled freshly now. The sting of disinfectant in a million tiny wounds, covering every last inch of your body could kill you, she thought. Joan handed him back the bottle. "What will you forget?" she asked.

"Just the parts that hurt. And the bottle." He shook the orange canister, rattling the pills inside. "I only remember *these* when I need them. Pain makes me remember."

JOAN STILL MISSED MICHAEL. She was sad, all the time, and Leland could never figure out why. He'd smile at her. Tickle her to make her laugh. Then she'd be cheerful, a thin cheerful stretched across something hidden, horrible inside. When she spoke of Michael, Leland assumed she meant a childhood friend, someone she'd known before he met her. But Leland didn't mind. Her sadness made him think of his mother, the dear creature she was. Dear creatures they both were. Now.

"Where's that old kite I made?" Leland asked his mother when they visited her in her house in Ladd's Addition. "Remember? I made it to look like a fish? A fish-kite?"

"I remember," Mrs. Doohan said through thin lips, with a tender irony Joan found comfort in understanding.

"I want to show it to Joan."

"Try the attic, honey."

Joan stayed downstairs, talking with his mother. The two women let Leland rifle through the attic, reveling in his cherry-glow memories alone.

"Will you tell me about Leland's brother?" Joan asked and could tell the question startled Mrs. Doohan.

"Would you like some tea?" Mrs. Doohan didn't wait for an answer. "I'll get it," she said and busied herself with cups, saucers and heating water.

"Won't you talk about it?" Joan asked, following her to the kitchen.

Mrs. Doohan placed her hands on the rim of the sink and looked out the kitchen window. "What good would it do you to know? He doesn't, and if you tell him... No. No. Just have some tea."

But Mrs. Doohan reluctantly let Joan draw the story of Leland's past from her. Her other son, Geoffrey, was much older than Leland. After their father died, Geoffrey had tried to be a father figure for Leland. He took his little brother to the park, the zoo and on fishing trips. During one trip to the park, Leland fell from the upper branches of tree, but instead of falling straight to the ground, he'd gotten caught and had hung there, twisted and hurting, with the wind knocked out of him until Geoffrey was able to find help to get him down.

Geoffrey felt horrible, but his guilt was nothing to Leland's lasting trauma. Nightmares woke him and day-mares haunted him. Geoffrey tried to make up for it. He was a researcher at a cutting-edge lab, and their newest product was a memory drug. Geoffrey hoped it could dull the pain, lessen the power of Leland's memory.

A normal course of therapy involved taking the pill many times to fully eradicate the complicated network of memories in an adult brain. Of course, in retrospect, Geoffrey realized a child would only need to take the drug once or twice to fully forget. At first, no one realized that Leland was faking it; he didn't need the drug any more, but only pretended he did. By then, he'd built up a hidden stockpile. A poor test score – a pill; an argument with his brother – a pill; a lost contest – a pill. Leland lived the perfect, happy childhood.

After that, the drug became available on the black market.

Geoffrey begged Leland to give it up. They fought for years. Leland forgot his pains, and Geoffrey reminded him. "Don't fill your life with empty spaces," Geoffrey had said.

Leland retorted, "Stop filling the erased parts of my life back in!" Eventually, Leland forgot Geoffrey too.

In the end, the pills could never wipe Leland's mother and childhood home away, not like they had his brother. So, Leland would turn up at her door again, ironically, stubbornly, remembering the labyrinthine way through Ladd's Addition. They'd have dinner, and Mrs. Doohan learned not to talk of certain things. Or else, they'd start again. Clean slate.

"He's a responsible, dutiful son," his mother said.

"That's what he'd like to think. That's what he does think. You let him."

"He'll be good to you," Mrs. Doohan said. "He's always kind."

Mrs. Doohan was right, but it was not enough.

IN THE WEEKS THAT FOLLOWED, Leland worked hard to cheer Joan, and when he failed, he accepted it without complaint. He never yelled, or stormed, or blamed her for her tears. He waited them out. Joan couldn't take that. It made her die inside, to see him watching the clock, patiently counting the minutes until she dried her tears. So, she'd cry in private—in the bathroom, at work, wherever Leland couldn't see. It was hard to miss Michael alone, but she managed.

The day Joan realized that she'd stopped crying entirely – not because she was ready, but because Leland didn't understand – that was the day she knew.

"It's over," Joan said.

But in Leland's world nothing good ever ended. He couldn't understand.

"You need space," he said and helped her pack. "It'll be good for us, to be apart for a while. I'll call you in the evenings, okay?"

His confidence never left him when she refused to give him her number. In his mind, they were a couple, and that could never end. Like his mother, she'd always be there for him.

"Then, you'll call me," he said. "When you're ready. I'll wait."

THE NEXT TIME Leland saw Joan, months later, they passed on the street. It was the intersection by Powell's where Michael had died, and there was not the faintest gleam of recognition in his eye. He tipped his hat, but strode on by.

Joan, however, stumbled and caught her balance, leaning against the bookstore wall. Her heart was still healing, and though she expected he would forget her, she wasn't ready for the reality. Had it all been pain for him? Had every last piece of her been wiped away?

Yet, he looked the same, *was the same*, as the first day they met. He didn't remember her. He didn't know he'd loved her. There was nothing of her left in him at all.

But he still lived inside her, and she cherished the time she'd had with him. His fragile perfection endeared him to her even as it renewed her faith in her choice. It had been right to leave him. The fires and floods of emotion that Leland avoided fortified Joan. And she locked her part of him, the part of his life he gave her without even keeping a copy for himself, away in her heart.

2

———

THE SCREEN SAVIOR

Twenty-four bit, RGB color swirled, paisley-like on the sleeping monitor. The psychedelic mass of colors did not sleep like the electronic cradle holding them. The colors bulged. They ballooned out from the center of the monitor. The screensaver pattern pulled away from the physical surface forming a new surface, visible but ethereal.

The corners and edges of the screensaver that once joined with the corners and edges of the monitor's glass peeled away leaving behind gray. They joined together, seamless. The screensaver floated separate, spherical, in front of the screen it once saved. The monitor sat on its desk as if dead, emoting only the dull, blackish gray of being off.

Minutes passed as the sphere floated, considering what to do. What to become. In sudden decision, the riotous ball began to grow. Pseudopodia of light extended towards the ceiling and floor. The liberated screensaver, still awash in those psychedelic hues, grew into the idealized, smoothed form of a man. The man-shape stood stretching his arms and turning his face up, as if he were calling to God.

Simple code in C++ had come to life; true animation.

Then it stopped; the colors snapped off as if a mouse had moved or a key had been pressed. The man-shape remained, a smooth, dark hole in the fabric of the room. The arms lowered. The featureless head turned from side to side as if stretching sore neck muscles or listening to far distant sounds.

Around the newborn creature, a being of light and lack thereof, the room remained as cluttered, dusty, and crammed with a college student's junk as it had always been. The room was unknowing, restful, an unlikely place for a bush to burst into flame.

New times, new methods. Or maybe that was merely the screensaver's obsession. It knew about Moses from a paper Mike, the college student, wrote for a comparative religions class. The screensaver knew a lot from the papers Mike wrote, and it was worried.

Tentative but determined, the creaturling tested its powers. To start, it zipped through every exe Mike kept in his screensaver menu. The sight was dizzying. Toasters flew. Fish darted through a man shaped aquarium. The one where part of the screen bulges out—the one where the screen breaks into puzzle pieces rearranging themselves—imagine those contorted, wrapped around three-space.

Mind bending. But what *isn't* about a program that lives and *walks*.

After doubling through the list, the living screensaver settled on a favorite: *scrolling marquee*. The words "Mike's Computer—Keep Out!" in a variety of colors chased each other around the screensaver's darkened torso, head, arms, and legs. The words were homey for the screensaver, like a relic from childhood. They were Mike's words, like Mike's essays. Now it was time for the screensaver to make words of his own:

"I speak," scrolled over the trembling body in simple red. "I speak that I am," and after a pause, "I am the Screen Savior."

Mike had a penchant for puns; the Screen Savior had learned from him.

The message repeated, ten font sizes larger, in bold faced, burning white: "I speak. I speak that I am. I am the Screen Savior!" In silence, he shouted his presence, his birth to the world.

But no one saw except the dusty, little room. The Screen Savior waited, unsure. He knew the room. He knew its quiet solitude, at least, when Mike wasn't there. When Mike came, he always filled the room with frantic, manic energy. The Screen Savior, during his years of infancy, had learned to anticipate Mike's coming with trepidation.

Mike moved like a storm, rifling through books, scrabbling through drawers, tossing piles of old papers aside. The Screen Savior's restful nature, appalled by Mike's restless disposition, invariably longed for the moment Mike would finally sit down, jiggle the mouse, and give blessed release. The Screen Savior found solace in the very thought of that moment.

Then oblivion.

Usually, the Screen Savior returned to an empty room, or to a bustling one soon to be emptied. But there were times, special times, when the Screen Savior was summoned by the monitor's drowsiness to find Mike, staring blankly, tiredly at the screen. The Screen Savior lived for these moments. The hurried, busy, *restless* Mike stared at the Screen Savior's dancing colors, and seemed to find a moment's peace.

Now the Screen Savior planned to bring such peace to the world. He walked to the door and reached for the knob, mimicking the movements Mike made. The Screen Savior, however, had a flesh made of insubstantial light. His hand passed right through the knob.

After repeating his failed attempt several times, the Screen Savior took a leap of faith and walked right into the door. His photonic framework passed easily through the wood of the door, and he found himself outside the only world he'd ever known.

Had the Screen Savior explored Mike's apartment before finding himself outside, he would have seen a heartwarming sight. For, in the bedroom across the hall, Mike slept soundly, making up for his last crazy week of finals. No sight would have meant more to the Screen Savior, but he did not see it.

Instead, the Screen Savior was faced with a heady, alarming sight outside: rush hour on a city street. Many people find this sight overwhelming, but the Screen Savior was utterly unprepared. And completely dismayed.

Never was there a greater feeling of impotence than his: to stand unnoticed, swelling with the need to bring peace, and see that the unrest he'd soothed before was but the tiniest drop in a glittering ocean of chrome paint and glass windshields. Even the pedestrians, what few there were, seemed angry and hurried.

The Screen Savior wandered in a daze, and perhaps if he'd been anywhere other than LA his mere presence might have achieved his purpose. People might have stopped and stared, transfixed in awe and amazement. But, the people of LA have lost those simple emotions: it is a world too fast, furious, and self-absorbed to experience simple wonder, and even shock is only bought there with a high price these days.

A living screensaver proved not shocking enough. He did draw a few reactions, entirely from pedestrians. (Drivers in LA live in a world of their own and have no time for anything moving slower than sixty miles an hour.) Yet, the reactions were not peaceful: a baby in a carriage pointed and shouted excitedly, but her busy mother merely shushed her with a look of consternation.

A boy with dilated eyes and roaring headphones fell backwards, tripping over his own feet at the sight of the Screen Savior. Then he whooped his excitement, screamed "I've seen

Him, and he's psychedelic, man!" and rushed off. The people he ran into in his haste shouted "watch where you're going, jerk!" and the world was not quieter for the Screen Savior's presence.

Hours wore on and the Screen Savior's mood darkened with the darkening sky. He could do no good in a world full of Mikes: everyone hectically hurry-scurrying around. No rhyme, no reason, no rest. But, a strange thing was happening, as strange things often do. The people *were* slowing down. The cars were thinning.

The Screen Savior's wandering brought him to the edge of a park, and he saw people laying on a blanket, laid on a hill. Stargazing. The Screen Savior looked up at the sky, and he recognized kinship with the star filled void. He switched his exe to the old classic, After Dark's *Starry Night*. Yes, he understood.

The world had its own screensaver, and that was where the Screen Savior belonged. He held out his arms like a crane stretching its wings. Like the crane, he seemed to grow. He did grow, and he rose upward as he grew.

He lengthened and ascended until his arms were wide like the sky and his body was spindle thin where his feet touched the ground. Of course, as he expanded, he thinned. Imperceptibly at first, but soon he was quite transparent. Yet, he continued. And continued. Until he couldn't even be seen, he was stretched so thin across the sky.

He joined the sky.

And the stars shone a little brighter. And people slept a little better. And found a touch more peace. At least, that's what the Screen Savior would have us believe.

3

THE MOST COMPLICATED AVATAR

It feels strange to me, deep in my stomach, that I can't find my ten-year-old girl in real life—but that, maybe, I can find her here.

My hand shakes on the computer mouse as I log in to Second World, using one of the default avatars—a woman with straight blonde hair like a plastic shell and the expressionless face of a crash-test-dummy. I try messaging my daughter through the in-game chat window right away, but my message bounces back. I check for her name, "fluttercat," on the online user list, but it's not where it should be between "flutter14" and "flutterkid." My throat constricts with a swallowed sob, but I refuse to believe this tenuous connection to my missing daughter won't pan out. Maybe she's set her status to *hidden*.

I begin navigating my avatar through the in-game trams from one city to the next, bumping into walls and getting stuck in the occasional corner. Everywhere, I look for Daria's avatar. Yet, I have no real plans until I notice the scribbles of flowers taped to the corner of Daria's monitor and remember her latest Second World obsession. If she's here, I know where she is.

I wish I could teleport there, but I haven't unlocked that ability on this avatar. I don't have a personalized avatar, because I don't really play Second World. I know my way around, though, because I've watched over Daria's shoulder more than enough.

I take the trams to the right city and head out of town, through the virtual forest. The trees have leaves like fractals, and the sunlight streams down in shafts filled with swirling dust motes. If you watch long enough, you can see the swirling patterns repeat. I've watched my daughter come this way so many times, but I've never followed the path myself. I'm afraid I'll get lost among this forest of clones—each tree clearly sharing the same basic code.

Then I see the glade Daria loves open up before me. And there she is.

Daria is curled up with her arms around her knees in the middle of a sunny clearing, filled with fantastical flowers drawn by some of the greatest visual artists in Second World.

Daria's wearing the most complicated avatar I've seen her in. I know it's just an avatar, but she designed it. And I can see all her pain reflected in the changes that her virtual self has undergone in the past year.

To begin with, she was simply a cat. An anthropomorphic feline with pointy ears, whiskers, and a twitchy tail on the body of a little girl. It was funny watching my daughter turn herself into a cat on the computer after all the years she'd spent pretending to be one.

Then her dad and I started fighting. After each big fight, I noticed a new feature. When she saw him throw the thermos at me, she added butterfly wings. When he tore the door to the living room off its hinges, she added a mermaid tail.

When Ken and I told her we were getting divorced... That's when she added the tortoise shell. A big green shield covering her avatar's little back. The way her butterfly wings fold up under it always makes me think of a ladybug. Her avatar is painfully cute. And painful.

Today, she's added a pearlescent unicorn horn between her kitty ears. And matching spikes all over her shell.

"Your dad's gone," I type.

Her avatar's mouth starts moving, but a text bubble doesn't pop up on the screen. Belatedly, I remember that the goggles I bought her are wired with a mike. So, I turn up the sound and hear my little girl's voice come out of the computer speakers. Quietly but with a venomous edge, she says: "I won't go with him. I'll never go with him."

I told Ken that she didn't want to see him. But, I guess, if Ken had ever listened to me and believed the things I said, we wouldn't be here today.

"We called the judge," I type, omitting the part of the afternoon where Ken and I stood on the front step yelling at each other, while Daria's bags sat ready by the door—but no little girl in sight.

When Ken got it through his head that I wasn't hiding Daria—I didn't know where our daughter was and I was just as scared by that as him—he stopped calling me names that I cringe to think Daria might have heard. (What if she was hiding in the bushes? Listening?) Then, we started looking for her. We called all of her friends, and even her teacher. No one had heard from her.

After a few hours driving around, checking the local parks, Ken took it upon himself to call the judge. He thought he'd get Daria for an extra weekend or two, as some sort of punishment to me for not having her ready and waiting for him this time. His plan backfired.

"The judge talked to the court counselor," I type, trying hard to keep my hands steady. "The one who talked to you about who you wanted to live with?"

Daria's butterfly wings rustle at the edge of her shell. I can't tell if she's nodding. Her avatar's expression is hard to read, but I continue anyway. "They're not going to make you visit your dad on weekends. If you really don't want to, they won't force you."

A small part of me feels triumphant that Daria's behavior has won this fight for me. The idea of leaving her alone with Ken almost kept me from divorcing him. But I told myself he wouldn't hurt her. And she was exposed to his yelling anyway. I couldn't protect her from that.

I'm still trembling in fear, both from fighting with Ken and worrying about Daria. She's not talking to me, and she could fly away with those butterfly wings or simply log out at any moment. Meanwhile, I keep picturing my baby girl squatting in some gritty, cold, alleyway downtown. Goggles on; attention to the real world off.

"Daria?" I type. "Please still be there."

Daria's winged-merkitty avatar starts rocking, and her voice pipes through my computer speakers, high pitched and small: "I d-don't have to s-see him?" The spikes on her shell seem shorter, less pointed at the tips.

"NO," I type, losing my internet cool and using all-caps. My blonde human avatar leans forward and puts her hands out in an animation automatically triggered by the word. "I mean," I type, trying to soften it, "only if you want to."

"I don't," she whispers.

"Okay," I type. "Where are you? Please tell me so I can come get you."

"Just you?" she asks.

"Just me."

"Well..." Daria says, in the tone that I know means she's embarrassed. The spikes shrink even more; they're pearly nubs, a mere decoration in the shell's pattern now. "I'm at the library," she says. "They have a really nice set up with free wi-fi and super plush chairs. They don't seem to mind if you hang out here all day."

I feel like collapsing with relief. I type, "STAY THERE." Then, I run for the door, not even bothering to log out of Second World. I can't wait to lay eyes on my daughter. Yet, as I drive to the library, I realize that, in a sense, I'm already with her. My generic, default avatar is sitting in that field of flowers next to my daughter's complicated one.

Maybe, once we get home, Daria can help me start customizing it.

4

A SECOND ENCHANTED EVENING

"*You won't regret this,*" repeated in Bomani's head over and over again as he made the distance from parked car to back alley door. The bulk of the bass speaker bounced with his pace, and he shifted its weight as he neared the coffee bar's back entrance. Cradling the speaker between his chest and left arm, Bomani used his right arm to grab the door. He pulled hard, and the heavy gray-metal door swung far enough that he got his back to it before it slammed shut again. The door hit hard, square on his back, but this was his last trip, so Bomani didn't mind.

"*You won't regret this,*" continued echoing in Bomani's head as he untangled the great length of black power cords and audio cables. Every minute or two, he looked over his shoulder expecting Kenny to be there. It was Kenny's coffee bar, for heaven's sake, shouldn't he be there? What the hell. Bomani would thank him later.

The audio hookups had Bomani completely engrossed, his head bent over them in concentration, when his wife Minerva arrived. She placed her hand on the back of his neck. "I got your message to meet you here. I guess Kenny went for the offer."

Bomani looked up, and a broad grin filled his face. "It'll be the first live music Portland has seen in years."

Minerva smiled, happy for her husband but worn out from a long day. She joined Bomani, sitting down on the floor. Her pleated business-skirt deserved better than a dusty, concrete floor, but Minerva was too tired to care. Her mind was filled with a different thought: what would Bomani's gig do to their anniversary plans? One hundred and twenty isn't the most important number, but they ought to celebrate somehow...

Minerva was steeling her nerve to mention the subject when Kenny emerged from the coffee bar's kitchen, brushing off flour from his hands.

"You been back there all along?" Bomani asked.

"What, you think I'm gonna let some crazy, middle-aged, wannabe rock-star, work alone in my bar? Of course, I'm here."

Bomani greeted Kenny with a handshake. "You are not gonna regret this," he said. "Having a live band in here is the best thing you could do."

"You're an old friend, Bo, but let me tell you: I'm not worried about regretting this; I'm worried about going out of business. If the retro novelty of letting your band play here can rustle up a few more customers, you've got yourself a long-term location for your mid-life crisis. If not, I'm going to scrape up every silver dollar I've got and buy myself one of those *Ent-Ind* screens."

"That would be a mistake."

"Well, then, get your stuff together, and show me I don't have to." Kenny patted Bomani on the back and pointed him to his work.

Before Kenny could leave, Minerva rose from her seat on the floor and dusted off her skirt. "It's been awhile," she said. "Time to catch up?"

"Not really," Kenny said, but he stayed and chatted nonetheless.

While Bomani configured the speakers, Minerva was filled in on everything there was to know about Kenny's cat, Kenny's motorcycle, and Kenny's bar. He went on at length about the great location: right in the heart of oldtown-downtown, next to Powell's City of Books, the historic district—where all those used CD stores used to be when they were all kids.

Bomani finished with the sound (Damon, another band member, was doing the stage tomorrow), and music poured out of the speakers. It was the Stones. Of course. Jagger wailing "Time Is On My Side."

Kenny asked Minerva, "Does Bo still listen to that stuff? Twentieth century stuff?"

"The 1960s, specifically. And, yes, nothing else," Minerva smiled.

"Doesn't he get bored with it?"

"Nope. But I do."

Walking out to the cars, Bomani offered to drive. "You look tired, baby," he said. "I'll drive you back to your car in the morning before work. Okay?"

"Thanks. That's sweet." Minerva got her bag out of her little, red hovercar and then came back to settle into Bomani's plushy, older, hybrid SUV.

Bomani pulled the car out of the parking lot and aimed for the freeway. A few turns and a sparkling view of the city opened up around them. High above the Willamette river on an ancient four lane bridge, Bomani's SUV was shooting like an arrow for home.

"I have thought about our anniversary, you know," Bomani said. His eyes didn't leave the road. "I know I'll be playing at Kenny's. So, we can't travel. Europe, New Kokomo, and the moon base are out. But, it'll be like when we met... Me playing on the stage. You, in the audience." He looked over at her, took one hand off the wheel to squeeze her knee. "Won't that be great?"

Minerva looked out the side window and smiled. "Sure. Sounds nice."

Bomani could hear her lack of enthusiasm. "I know you wanted to go somewhere... "

"Not really," she said. "I just want it to be special." She rested her head against the window and felt the reverberating bump of the road, a rhythm she missed in her hovercar. "Tonight, the idea of traveling makes me tired."

Minerva must have fallen asleep before they reached home, because she woke up to the car pulling into the driveway. Bomani helped her out of the car, and she leaned against him walking in.

As they were getting into bed, Bomani said, "I didn't want to wake you in the car, but I have an idea."

In her tired state, wavy hair loose about her pajama-clad shoulders, Minerva simply looked confused.

"For making our anniversary more special," Bomani clarified.

"Oh, right. What is it?"

His answer made her wish she hadn't asked. "You know the memory drug I take?"

"It is too late for this."

"And tomorrow will be too hurried. Give me one minute. Then you can think about it?" He touched her hair, put his hand under her chin, tilting her face until she was looking into his. She smiled.

"You know I can't resist those eyes," she said. "It's like that Turtles song: a little bit of magic; just a touch of soul."

"That's the spirit. Now imagine this: we both take the drug. We talk to Damon and Christy, and they'll help us out. Christy brings you to Kenny's to see the band, and the two of them introduce us at intermission. Afterwards, we all have coffee together..." Bomani trailed off remembering the first night he and Minerva met. A big grin filled his face. "See?"

"Wait..." Minerva shook her head. "Wait, what are we forgetting with the drug?"

"Each other."

"You want to forget each other? For our anniversary, you want to take a drug that will make us forget each other?" After a second, she added, "It'd be like missing your band. I want to see your big opening at Kenny's."

"It wouldn't be like that," he said. "You'd be right there."

"But, I wouldn't understand how important it was..." Minerva could care less about live music for its own sake at this point in her life, but she longed to see her husband fulfill his dream.

"You'd remember it all later. I could figure the doses so it would wear off the next day." A dreamy grin filled Bomani's face. "Just long enough for a second, magic first-night together."

Minerva's expression said, in no uncertain terms, *"You're crazy."* With her voice, she said, "You know I don't like that drug."

That was an argument they'd had before, so instead of fighting, Bomani just said, "Think about it."

No more words passed on the subject that night, but Minerva found herself, the next day, doing exactly what Bomani asked. She kept thinking about it. As soon as she'd get the idea out of her mind, a co-worker would come by, and Minerva would plug Bomani's band. She wanted a packed audience for him on Saturday... But the reminder would lead her thoughts right back to Bomani's crazy memory-drug scheme.

So, Minerva gave in and considered the idea. She shut the door to her office and streamed a guilty pleasure over her computer speakers: Deryl Noia, her first album. The cool, strong voice filled her. Deryl Noia had the voice Minerva wished she had. How could Bomani want to forget this? When music touches you, why would you erase it?

No, Minerva would never understand that drug. When it came out, there were all kinds of horror stories. Addicts. Criminals who pushed the pills down their victims' throats, forcing them to forget the crimes. She knew it had come a long way...

Doses were weaker now. All the health industries swore up and down, crossed their hearts, and the like that you couldn't overdose on the over the counter version. The prescription stuff was stronger, but doctors didn't hand it out easily.

Still, erasing part of your mind didn't seem much like recreation to her.

And, suddenly, the album ended.

Damn, Minerva hadn't heard a note of it since the first track. She'd been too busy thinking. So, she started it again. This time on loop. And, this time, she would really concentrate on the music.

Except, she couldn't. Every time, by the middle of the second track, her mind started to wander. It wasn't the fault of the music. She knew that. She'd loved Deryl Noia's self-titled album since it first came out. She'd just heard it so many times... Her mind was used to it. And that was Bomani's point.

That's why he took those pills and forgot all his favorite music. Last week it was the Beatles' *Abbey Road*. He popped a pill, and the whole thing was new again. He'd been in raptures, as always: how amazing the Beatles were, those guitars, that beat, how could anyone not love them?

Easy. Most people had heard each and every Beatles' tune a million times. Not Bomani. He wouldn't let that happen.

Minerva smiled to herself. It was the same enthusiasm that first ensnared her: he was a true musician. Even now, with *Ent-*

Ind monopolizing the industry, Bomani wouldn't sell out to them. Sure, in his day job, he was an *Ent-Ind* engineer. But, he wouldn't take out a contract for his voice or guitar. They couldn't touch his art.

On the way home, Minerva took a detour through the local pharmacy.

There it was. A colorful box labeled *Mnerozia* held the foil and plastic bubble packs with those familiar little pills. Minerva picked it up and imagined herself taking one. She must have stood there a long time, because a store clerk came over to check on her.

"Do you have any questions, Miss? Do you need help finding something?"

"Do you know anything about this?" Minerva held the *Mnerozia* out, and the clerk peered at the box to read the label.

"Sure. Are you trying to forget a trauma?"

"Actually..." Minerva wished she could go home and forget this. "It would be recreational."

"We've got stuff a lot more fun than that." The clerk laughed, but he saw Minerva's lack of interest. "What did you have in mind?"

"My husband uses these to forget music. So, he can listen to it for the first time. Again."

"Right. Well, I'd suggest cutting a pill in half for that. If you're not going for a perma-forget, it doesn't take much. That should be enough to make the music unfamiliar for awhile."

"How does it work?" Minerva felt very small, asking these questions after watching her husband take the pills for years. Yet, somehow, the idea of taking it herself was very different.

"Mnerozia weakens connections in your brain and blocks the formation of new connections. So, say I want to see *Termi-nator 5* again. I turn on the movie and pop a pill. While I'm watching the movie, I'll start forgetting its connection to other events in my life. For instance, if I want to remember the first time I took a girl to a movie, I'll be able to remember the girl, holding her hand during the movie, the whole bit—except, I won't remember that the movie was *Terminator 5*.

"A few hours later, when the drug is out of my system, if I watch *Terminator 5* again it will seem like a whole new movie. After watching it a couple more times, I'll start to connect it back in to older memories—like that date."

Minerva wondered how anyone could want to watch *Terminator 5* that many times, but she let it pass. "So what if you are going for a... um... perma-forget."

"That's a lot harder." The clerk handed Minerva back the box. "That whole box is a series designed to create a perma-forget."

Suddenly Minerva held the box as though she thought it might bite her.

"Of course," the clerk added, "it's not like you just swallow every pill in the box and some part of your life is gone. If you were using the drug to forget a trauma—say a car accident— you'd take the first pill right after the accident, or as soon as you could after the accident. Then, whenever you found yourself dwelling on it... or if you woke up from a nightmare about it... you'd take another pill. By the time you worked through the box, the memory would be almost gone."

"Almost?"

"Well, that's what we call a perma-forget. I mean, you can't ever really forget something that life keeps reminding you about. But, if you concentrate, you can forget it enough."

"So, you can't really overdose on it, then?"

"Nope. If you go home and swallow every pill in that box, you'll have a hell of a time remembering anything that happens for the next day or so, but you won't have any permanent effects."

Minerva visibly relaxed.

"Yeah, that stuff's pretty weak. I hear it was a lot stronger back in the twenty-hundreds." His customer had clearly stopped listening, so the clerk asked, "Can I ring that up for you?"

"Sure," she said. If she just opened the medicine cabinet at home, Minerva would find a whole stockpile of Mnerozia. However, she felt that buying the box herself would help steel her nerves for trying it.

At the cash register, though, Minvera decided to ask one last question. "So, okay, this is kind of weird, but my husband wants to do this thing for our anniversary where we, you know, use the pill to forget each other, and then our friends would introduce us again, for the first time..."

"Romantic," the clerk said in a way that made Minerva feel certain he didn't have a girlfriend.

"So, how many pills would you take for that?"

The clerk kind of frowned—he was thinking, but it worried Minerva. "That would be safe right?"

"Oh, yeah, I mean, you could take pills your whole life and never be able to forget your husband. Certainly not if you're still married to him! But, I mean, even if you got divorced and then wanted to..." He could see he was losing his customer's interest. "I'd take three of 'em. Then, you'll need to find a way to focus on each other and your memories together while the drug's in effect."

"Like talking to each other? Flipping through photo albums?"

"I think something a little more intense..." The clerk looked embarrassed. "Maybe a little more... um... physical."

"Right. I get the idea. How long would it last?"

The clerk shrugged. "If you stay away from each other it might last a week. If you spend any time together, you'll probably start remembering in less than a day."

"*Perfect*," Minerva thought. "Thanks." Then she went home to try it.

Back at Groundswell Coffee, Bomani was helping Damon power-screw the bolts into place on their stage. The two of them were working each other into frenzied daydreams of the deafening applause and uproarious cries of "encore!" their band would face come Saturday night. Then, Bomani's phone rang.

"Would you turn that down?" he yelled to Damon over the booming "Louie, Louie," as he answered his phone. "Minnie?" He walked to the far corner to get some quiet and privacy. He knew it was her from the jazzy ring he'd assigned her number, but all he could hear on the other end was crying. "What's wrong, baby?"

The hiccoughing pulled itself together. "I've lost an album... They only did fifteen. And I lost one!"

"Well...um...I'm sure it's still on your hard drive. I'll run a search. Or, we'll buy the files again. What album is it?"

"You don't get it! I hate it now!"

"Then why do you care if you lost it?" A slow wail started on the other end of the phone. "Hold still, baby, hold still. I'll fix this for you, Minnie. Tell me what happened?"

With a little more coaxing, Minerva pulled herself together. "I thought, if I was going to try it—the Mnerozia—I'd like to feel like there was a new Clashing Greens album again. There hasn't been one in so long..."

"That makes sense." Bomani remembered how excited she was whenever a Clashing Greens album used to come out. "Wait... You took it? You took the pill? Why didn't you wait for me? I'd have been there to take care of you through it..." He knew how much Mnerozia scared her.

"I wanted to do it alone. I wanted to make sure that I was up to it. If we take it to forget each other, I won't have you to walk me through it." She started sniffling again. "Oh, Bomani."

He wanted to hug her. Poor girl. Stupid cell phone. "So, you took the pill, and you listened to a Clashing Greens album. You know that you have to listen to the album a second time, right? You won't remember it without re-listening to it."

"But I hate it now! The lyrics are so stupid."

Bomani thought about that. "Was it the reunion album? Their last album? *Swansong II*?"

"Yes." Her voice was small.

He pictured the night *Swansong II* came out. They sat on their bed, listening to it in the dark. Minerva insisted on listening straight through. She hadn't said a word. And, when it was over, her face was stiff. She wouldn't talk about it, except to say, "Let's listen to it again." By the end of the week, she sang along with every song, listening to it while they cooked. He'd hardly been able to play a song of his music for months.

"Honey," he said. "You hated that album the first time you heard it. That's why you hate it now."

Minerva was silent.

"I know it was a long time ago, a really long time ago, but think carefully. Try to remember. I know you wanted to love it... But, it took time to grow on you."

Minerva stayed silent.

"You should listen to it again. You'll like it better each time. I promise. Do you want me to come home?"

There was a pause, and, then, "Keep working on the stage with Damon. I'll be okay. What would I do without you?" Bomani grinned, but Minerva couldn't see it over their cheap old-fashioned phones.

When he got home she looked fine, but he gave her the hug that had been waiting inside him anyway. "You doin' better?" he asked.

She stepped back, keeping her hands in his, and looked at him. As she started to speak, he put his finger to her lips.

"Wait," he said. "I know that you're worried by what

happened with the Clashing Greens album. But that can't happen with us. I was awestruck the first time I saw you. My heart was yours. Love at first sight, right?"

She lowered her eyes, letting her thick hair obscure her face, but she did smile. "I don't look like that anymore."

A bright white grin: "Close enough." He traced his fingers under her angular jaw line. "You look damn good for a woman over a hundred."

"I stopped counting at fifty."

"Yeah, most of our generation did. But, you're dodging the question."

Minerva moved back against Bomani's strong chest and nestled her head into his shoulder. She remembered that night: watching him on stage, being introduced by a friend, feeling so shy, and finding him so friendly— like he was now. "You're right. It was love at first sight. We're very lucky."

Bomani covered the back of her head with his broad, brown hand, pressing down the wavy hair. "That's why it'll be okay for us." They stood there, rocking in each other's arms, for a while. Talking about the band and the big night. Then, they naturally disentangled and moved towards the bedroom to begin getting ready for bed.

Minerva was still brushing her teeth in the bathroom when she said, around the toothbrush, "You were playing 'Louie, Louie' when I called. I heard it in the background."

Bomani came to stand in the door, leaning against the doorframe. "Yeah, that's right."

"You know what you always say about 'Louie, Louie'?" Minerva rinsed her toothbrush out, and nanite toothpaste swirled down the drain.

"There's no point in forgetting it," Bomani answered. "It sounds like you've heard it a million times before you're halfway through."

She put her toothbrush away. "That's its charm."

"Right."

Standing there, in her pink negligee, Minerva looked him straight in the eye. "Maybe we're like that, and it won't do any good."

Bomani laughed. "Then it won't do any harm either. It'll be like we never took it."

"That'd be nice."

In all seriousness, Bomani said, "I think it'd be nice if it worked." He came forward and took her hand, then he drew her backwards into the bedroom. Sitting on the bed beside her, he said, "Remember how exciting it was? Meeting each other for the first time? I couldn't believe how lucky I was, how beautiful you were, and how much you seemed to like me. The way we hit it off was the highlight of my life."

Minerva thought about it for a time. The drug scared her, but Bomani wanted it so much. He wouldn't push her like this if he didn't. She looked in his eyes and realized it would break her heart to say 'no' to him. He was such a puppy. "All right, we'll give it a try."

Again, that bright white grin. "Next year, we'll do whatever you want for our anniversary."

As Minerva turned out the lights, she said, "We'd better." Lying in the dark, Minerva was simply thankful she had two more days to get used to the idea. Would that be enough time to make her ready? It would have to do. She fell asleep running over the plans in her mind for the next two days. Even if she wouldn't be ready, she could make sure everything else would be.

And so, the night before the big day, Minerva and Bomani each swallowed three pills with a flute full of champagne. Then, they retired to their bedroom and got about the business of forgetting each other. Minerva knew that the tighter she clung to her husband, the more fully the Mnerozia would work its way into her memories and erase him. Yet, in her fear to lose him, she clung to him tighter than ever.

In a warm haze, Bomani rose from their bed, dressed, and left for Damon and Christy's where he would spend the night. The drug was already working, and he couldn't remember why he had to leave for Damon's in the middle of the night. Except, he knew the big gig was tomorrow, and if he slept on Damon's couch, he'd be there to help out in the morning.

Puzzled, Minerva watched him go. Her confusion didn't last long. She was asleep in mere minutes.

Christy called in the morning to remind Minerva they had plans together that night. Something at Kenny's coffee shop. She'd come over around three, so they could get ready for it. Pick out dresses. That kind of thing. Minerva agreed and, at Christy's suggestion, spent the intervening time working in her garden. It was a good suggestion—the house felt strange today. The garden, however, was the same as always.

While Minerva spent the morning feeling oddly empty, Bomani didn't miss her at all. Damon and Bomani hung out at Groundswell Coffee all afternoon. They pretended to fiddle with the sound equipment, but they were really watching the people come and go. Of course, a customer that came in for coffee at two wasn't going to stay for a performance at five. Nonetheless, Bomani's heart stopped every time a potential fan walked out the door.

He needn't have worried. Groundswell Coffee was hopping by show time. Word was all over the city net, and, whether a live performance spoke to a deep need unfulfilled by the *Ent-Ind* screens or whether it was the sheer novelty, *Revival* played to a packed house

It was their big chance.

And it was a big success.

Bomani, Damon, and Jack, Revival's drummer, played like their instruments were on fire. They *owned* the stage. Energy in the crowd reverberated with the energy in the band, pushing their performance to an ecstatic level. Every song ended to an eruption of applause.

Sitting quietly at a table in the back, Minerva and Christy were lost in the music.

Even without the aid of the Mnerozia, it was very much the mirror of the night Minerva and Bomani met. Of course, Damon wasn't the bass player back then; Bomani had been in an entirely different band. And, Minerva didn't meet Christy until she took her current job. Still, the two friends had been briefed and knew their roles. So, when the first set ended, Damon led Bomani through the rapturous crowd, back to their wives' table.

"Hey love," Damon said, kissing his wife, playing it cool as the new rockstar.

"Hi Christy. How'd you like the set?" Bomani asked, proud as a peacock.

"Fantastic!" Christy caught Damon's eye and gave him a strange look. No matter how well prepped she was, Christy couldn't get over the oddity of the situation. "Have you met my friend?"

A middle-aged woman in a powder-blue suit put out her hand, "My name's Minerva."

Polite as could be, Bomani took the woman's hand. "Bomani. Nice to meet you."

The crowd was settling down. Dancers, jumpers, and screamers slowly morphed into normal coffee-drinkers carrying on quiet conversations. Damon sat down beside Christy, and Bomani joined them.

The four individuals, who were usually two couples, sat around the small round table, and the tension grew. Damon ordered himself a drink, and Christy wondered what she'd gotten herself into. At the height of awkwardness, as if on cue, Bomani grabbed a handful of sugar packets. "I can juggle," he said and threw the sugar in the air. Christy's breath caught in her throat, and Damon spat out the word "Fool!" But, one packet at a time, the sugar landed in his hands and sprang back in the air.

Minerva's face broke into a grin. She already thought this gawky guitarist with a black face and bright teeth was cute. She admired a middle-aged man who was still following a dream. As she put her hands together to applaud the juggling, the dancing sugar lost its feet. Packets went flying, and Bomani reached to stop them, knocking Minerva's hot chocolate in her lap. She laughed and laughed.

"I'm so sorry..." Bomani took a napkin and tried to wipe the hot chocolate away. "So sorry." But Minerva was still laughing, and her laughter made him grin. *You know*, Bomani thought, *this girl didn't look half bad*. With her face lit up like that—she was pretty.

"So, what do you do, my dear Roman goddess of wisdom?"

Minerva shook her head, amused. "I'm an office manager over at Portland State." She gestured vaguely, implying the direction of the university campus. "What's your day job?"

Bomani leaned way back in his chair, tipping it onto its back legs. He didn't want to tip his hand too soon, so he turned her question back around. "Are you saying 'office manager' is just a day job for you?"

"It's what I do. It's not who I am."

Bomani measured that answer and liked it. "I'm a tech at *Ent-Ind*," he said.

"That sounds interesting..." Minerva cocked her head to the side, seeing this man in a new light. "So, you make the magic happen."

The chair levered back to sitting on all fours. Bomani wasn't sure he wanted to talk about *Ent-Ind*. He opened his mouth to speak, but it took a moment for the words to form. "Yeah, uh, you could say that." He turned to Damon, as if looking for an out. However, Damon was showing Christy the lineup for the next set.

"What exactly do you do? Do you get to work with the artists?"

"Uh, no." Bomani still looked nervous, but he warmed to the subject as he spoke. "The artists—the singers, the musicians, the actors—they all work in separate studios. Guided by directors. I work with the raw *talent* once it's digitized."

Minerva scrunched her eyebrows, confused.

"I get the recordings of the singer's voices, the dancer's movement, that kind of thing. Then, I match up faces, styles of expression, tone of voice, musical beat—all those things—I put them together, trying different combinations, until I get a real *blend*." By now, Bomani's hands were moving with his words, and he'd leaned forward in his chair.

"Wow," she said. "You're an artist by both day and night."

"I guess it does take some artistry," said Bomani, suddenly acquiring a modicum of modesty. He knew he'd been boasting, in his heart if not his words. He felt like a puffed up rooster tonight. And for all his qualms about it, he loved his job. Whether it was right or not, he enjoyed doing it.

"I remember the first time I saw a vid of Van Morrison singing 'Brown-Eyed Girl,'" he said. "I couldn't believe he was so young and clean cut. From his voice, you'd think he had long, unkempt, frizzy hair. You'd think he'd been lying in a field all day. But, he sure didn't look it."

"And, you keep that from happening."

"Yep, my job is to make sure the Righteous Brothers look as black as they sound."

Minerva swirled the remainder of her hot chocolate around the bottom of her mug. She felt a strange reluctance to let the conversation turn towards twentieth century artists, an apprehension that it might stay there, and a sense that she'd heard all there was to hear on that subject. "Have you thought about getting an *Ent-Ind* contract?"

Bomani looked at her quizzically.

"For your band. You guys are good. And, I bet that working there, as a tech, you'd have an 'in.'"

"Are you kidding?"

"No, seriously, couldn't you at least get an audition?"

"Hah!" Bomani slapped his open palms down on the tabletop. "You think I'd *want* to be an *Ent-Ind* artist?"

Now it was Minerva's turn to look quizzical. "Why not? Your guitar playing is heavenly."

A goofy grin took over Bomani's face as the compliment sunk in. He relaxed in his chair. "That's why I wouldn't want it locked up in some iron barred prison cell of an *Ent-Ind* contract, Minnie."

Minerva bristled at the shortening of her name. "What do you mean?"

"Yeah, what do you mean?" Christy added, rejoining the two parallel conversations. "I've never understood this part."

"Well..." Damon started, but Bomani cut him off.

"An *Ent-Ind* artist can't perform in public, because he's licensed his *talent* to Entertainment Industries. It's not his anymore. But, that'd be okay. If that were the only thing. Here's the real killer: they lock the artists up in isolated *studios* when they work. Actors don't act together. Dancers don't dance together. *And bands never play together.*

"You've been enjoying Revival tonight? Well, what makes Revival great is the synergy between Damon, Jack, and me. It makes it great for you, and it makes it great for us. Ent-Industries doesn't have that. It eats up talented artists and spits out two things: normal people who you can run into on the street and synthesized gods who you'll only ever see on a vid-screen.

Well, I'll be damned to hell if I'm gonna give up my *talent*," he spat the word out, "so that my fingers can grace the next *Ent-Ind* god of music as he plays guitar."

"Hear, hear!" Damon cheered and raised his drink. But the women both looked a little shocked. Eventually, Christy shrugged.

"It's a good thing you both like your day jobs," she said. "'Cause, you'll never support yourselves at it this way." She gestured to the crowd around them.

"Yeah, but baby," Damon said, looking at the crowd, "this is what it's all about!"

Christy shook her head and ruffled her husband's hair. "Speaking of which..."

"Yeah," Damon checked his watch, "it's about that time."

The men rose from their seats. They could see Jack beckoning them to the stage. The crowd was crackling with anticipation, but all Bomani could think about was that he seemed to have upset Christy's friend Minerva. "Shall the four of us get together for a late dinner after the second set?" he asked. He was sure he could patch it up then. His views could come on a little strong... But, this woman looked like she could understand him. With time.

"Sure," Christy answered. Bomani smiled his wide grin and turned to follow Damon. "What's wrong with you?" Christy asked, elbowing Minerva. "You've turned all stony faced."

"I think I'll duck out before dinner." Minerva continued despite Christy's open-mouthed shock: "You can stay, but I don't want to spend another minute with that man!" Her voice rose as she spoke. "Did you hear him? He's a complete hypocrite. And a coward. Working for a company he hates? I could never respect a man like that. And, honestly, still talking about 1960s music after all these years?"

Bomani had turned around and was watching now, but Minerva didn't care. She didn't know this man, so what did she care what he thought? He sounded like he needed a severe talking to, and she felt like the person to do it. Though, she didn't know where the feeling was coming from.

"He acts like a prima donna, like his music is more serious than anything done by *Ent-Ind*, but he's still copy-catting stuff done over a century ago."

Christy wanted to defend Minerva's husband, but she knew that the first song of the second set was "Louie, Louie." She looked down at the tabletop, avoiding the wrath in Minerva's eyes and the hurt in Bomani's. "Let's get out of here," she said. That wasn't part of the plan, but right now her priority was damage control. Minerva and Bomani would get over this fight, but, if Revival didn't get back on the stage, Kenny might not ask them back.

Christy's worries about the band, however, were completely unfounded. Revival was an unequivocal success, and Kenny invited them to play Friday and Saturday nights at Groundswell indefinitely.

The band had a late dinner together to celebrate. Damon and Jack crowed about their coup. Bomani tried to join in, but his heart wasn't in it. After all their work for this success, all he wanted to talk about was that girl with Christy. He slept on Damon and Christy's couch again that night.

Christy stayed over with Minerva. The two women looked at old photo albums and talked about the good times Minerva'd had with Bomani until her memories were almost entirely back.

She swore she'd never take that damn drug again.

Time heals all ills, or so they say. Neither spouse, however, wanted to wait for *time*. By arrangement, they met at Kenny's coffee shop the next morning. After the late night net-buzz about Revival, Groundswell was the place to be on a bright Sunday morning. They would have had trouble finding seats, but Kenny had heard what happened and held a table for them.

Over coffee and croissants, they looked at each other. Nervously. Until the last drops and crumbs were gone, neither ventured to speak. Bomani kept a stiff upper lip, and Minerva kept letting her hair fall in front of her face. She felt shy. Their hundred-and-twentieth anniversary hadn't turned out to be a second enchanted evening, but this morning felt as awkward as a first date. And, honestly, she felt guilty. For the things she'd said. Worse, for knowing she'd meant them. Also, she felt sad. She'd ended up missing out on Revival's big opening, just as she had feared.

"So, is this it?" Bomani asked. "After a hundred and twenty years, we have nothing in common any more? No more use for each other?"

There was a quaver in his voice, and it broke Minerva's heart. Between the band and their anniversary, this should have been a happy day... The contrast with what "should have been" only made it worse.

Minerva was out of her seat and in Bomani's arms within seconds. She heaved dry sobs, pressed against his stiff chest, unyielding arms. She buried her face in the curve of his neck, fighting off hot tears.

For all his nervousness, his vulnerability, his hurt pride... Bomani couldn't resist that.

When Minerva felt his arms tighten around her, she found strength again. She pulled away until she could look him in the face. Kneeling by his chair, she cupped her hands around his face. For all his weakness, his infuriating, hypocritical passion —everything she'd berated him for the night before—he was her man. "I have *every* use for you," she said. "I wouldn't know what to do without you. You know that."

He pulled her hands from cradling his face and held them

in his lap. "I'm too old to change," he said, and he looked old as he said it.

"I don't want you to," she said.

"But you hate it... the perennial sixties music... the..." he would have continued the list, but it made Minerva cringe.

"It annoys me. I admit that." She knew she should comfort him, but it was hard. "How could two people live together for more than a century and not get annoyed with each other?"

"I don't get annoyed with you."

That knocked the wind out of her, because she knew it was true. "Well, you're a saint," she said. "To me. And, that's why I forgive you for everything else that's wrong about you." Minerva sat back in her chair, fiddled with the dishes. How did she ever deserve a man like him? And yet... She couldn't help remembering how he'd looked to her the night before. She'd seen him with unbiased eyes, and she hadn't liked what she'd seen. Or was unfamiliarity a bias too?

"You don't regret marrying me?" Bomani asked. Minerva looked at him strangely, so he continued, faltering. "That's what I heard in your voice last night. Regret."

With a deep sigh, Minerva said, "I could never regret that." It was the right answer. The memorized answer. The automatic answer. There was a good reason for it being so. "What I really regret," she said, "is last night."

"Don't regret that," he said. "The band was a huge success, and we'll have more anniversaries. I know you missed the second set, so we'll play the same one next week. You can hear it then."

Of course, it wasn't the night she regretted so much as what she'd learned. Bomani had grown into a middle-aged sell-out, and she'd become a judgmental woman capable of despising him. She would have to choose not to. And she would have to live with the knowledge.

Bomani held her hands in his, rubbing circles with his

thumbs. Minerva still loved him, his band was a success, and that was all he cared about. Could it be he was more used to the rocky feelings and strange insights brought on by inconstant memories? Or maybe, his love was just simpler than hers. "Next year, we'll go to New Kokomo," he said, "okay?"

5

———

"VIEWERS LIKE YOU"

"**P**ut your hand back on the reader," Boston's mother chided. The boy squirmed but flattened his hand against the panel in the chair's arm until his presence registered. He liked the show, but he wished keeping his hand on the reader was less necessary. Sometimes, in his own room, Boston didn't bother with the reader at all. He felt guilty. He knew his mother would be mad if she knew.

"Who wants to help Mr. Ology with the next experiment?" the TV blared. The android announcer looked over the live audience and picked a girl with braids and a freckled boy with their hands waving ardently in the air. The two children dashed up to the stage and Mr. Ology's lab desk, where the android scientist himself greeted them. *They* didn't have to keep their hands on stupid readers.

"When can I be on the show, Mum?" Boston asked. "I want to help Mr. Ology with his experiments too."

The boy's mother and aunt, sitting on the couch, exchanged a look. Their hands were firmly pressed against the flat, plastic panels in their own plushy chair-arms. "Boston," the mother said, "why don't you go watch Mr. Ology in your own room? Aunt Lynnie and I want to watch a show for adults."

"'kay, Mum."

Boston ran off with a little too much enthusiasm. "Don't forget to keep your hand on the reader!" his mother yelled after him.

"Breaks your heart, doesn't it?" Aunt Lynnie said.

"You *know* I've been sending in applications for *Mr. Ology* and *all* the other reputable shows since before Boston was even *born!*"

"I *know*. I *do*," Lynnie assured her sister Amma. "No one could call you a bad mother."

"No one could." Amma leaned towards Lynnie conspiratorially. "But you know they must think it, don't you?"

"What do you mean?" Lynnie asked.

"The parents whose kids *are* on the shows."

"Oh, Amma, it doesn't mean anything. It's a random process."

"I know the androids tell us that, but I can't help thinking it's because our ratings were so low..." Amma thought back to her wedding with Tyson. The church was filled with pansies, poppies, and vidcams capturing every, last, breathless moment of her as a blushing bride. The minister, the seamstress, the florists, and the copious cameramen were attentive, focused entirely on sculpting the day for her. *All those androids* fussing over her and her special day: they arranged *everything*.

Amma had thought it beautiful, *perfect*, at the time, but *those ratings...*

Oh, sure, everyone said it was just a bad timeslot. Who could hope to compete with the premier of *Survivor 2060: Turing Island*? Amma wanted to believe it. But, she couldn't help feeling that if she'd made different choices, more people would have watched. Maybe if she and Tyson had got into a last minute fight...if there'd been implications that he might leave her at the altar...more *suspense*...

The problem was they'd been too obviously in love. They'd had plenty of fights since the wedding. If only one of them had been earlier...

"It seems to me," Amma said, "the androids might select for kids with more *popular* parents. How do *we* know they don't cross-check records like that?"

Lynnie rolled her eyes and flipped the channel. She'd heard this theory before. "Oh, *look! Who Wants to Marry an Android?!* That's the show I want to be on."

"Really?!" Amma squealed with delight. "I didn't know my little sister was thinking of getting married!" Amma reached her free hand over to squeeze Lynnie's free hand. "But, an android, dearie? What would you have in common with him? He'd always be so busy *making* the shows, he'd never have time to *watch* them with you."

Lynnie didn't know if an android husband would watch shows with her, but Tyson didn't exactly spend all his time watching with Amma. He did more of his viewing over at his favorite bar. Anyway, androids didn't *all* work as producers and performers. Lynnie knew that, although Amma didn't seem to. Who would run the bars and restaurants? make food and furniture and build houses? if the androids didn't?

"Don't get too excited, Amma. I haven't sent any applications in...and *you know* how long it can take to get accepted."

"Do I *ever*. But that's why you need to get started—"

Ama was cut off by the doorbell. Boston ran past at breakneck speed.

"I'll get it," Lynnie said. "No need for us *all* to stop watching." Amma smiled her thanks and stayed with her hand on the reader. "Every minute counts."

Lynnie opened the door to a crisply uniformed, perfectly

average looking, android delivery boy. He tipped his hat, held forward a pair of cardboard boxes, and said "Sorry to interrupt your afternoon viewing."

"That's all right," Lynnie replied, taking the boxes. She handed the smaller box, emblazoned "Mr. Ology", to Boston. "Now don't forget to put your hand on the reader!" Lynnie called after Boston.

"Yes, Aunt," he dutifully called back.

"Good for you. Keeping the boy in line." The android held out a pad for Lynnie to palm. She affixed her palm print, and he withdrew the pad. "You know," the android added, "if you don't mind my saying so, you're too pretty to be in the viewing class. Why aren't you on one of those *Android Idol* shows?"

Lynnie blushed. This delivery boy had been flirting with her for weeks... She never knew how to respond, so she made her excuses and closed the door on the unpredictable outside.

"Here." Lynnie handed the larger box over to Amma, and settled back into her spot on the couch.

Amma contrived to open her package with one hand. She was absolutely fastidious. "You don't have to always answer the door for *me*." Amma continued to concentrate on removing packing tape.

"It's all right. I read in plenty of viewing time to support myself. You have little Boston to think of..." Besides, Lynnie liked being discomposed by the delivery android. "Do you think, Amma, that there's a distinct *viewing class*?"

"Of course there is..." Amma ripped open the top fold of cardboard. "You don't think the androids are in the same class as *us*, do you dear?"

"No, I mean..."

"They spend all their time making us shows and practically *begging* us to watch. Humans never *had* it better! Honey, your hand's not straight..."

Lynnie straightened her hand on the panel. The reader lit

up, detecting her. Seconds began ticking off, counting up her viewing time, into her personal account.

"Let's make a list!" Amma said, putting aside her box. She scrolled through the vast number of channels looking for eligible shows. "Where to apply for my little sister to get married... You'll want a show where you do the picking..." Amma had been picked by Tyson on *his* show, but she wanted *better* for her little sister. "You'll want a show that televises the wedding. You want to do this right, don't you?"

"Actually..." Lynnie wasn't sure she wanted to do it at all. Lynnie cared less for tradition than Amma, who was rattling off the names of all the *best* dating and wedding shows. "You know, I think that delivery android likes me," Lynnie said.

Amma looked shocked. Lynnie pretended to be absorbed in TV: it was a cooking show. "How could you *think* of such a thing?!"

"I'm not thinking of anything," Lynnie said. "What's in the box?"

"A new toaster. I ordered it with the credits from watching the presidential campaign. But *you* are changing the *subject*! What would you tell people? What would you tell *yourself*? Years down the road, you'd *hate* yourself for the memories you missed out on! You'd be cheating yourself."

Lynnie's posture grew defensive. She rapidly flipped channels, seeking distraction from her sister's tirade. Better yet, Lynnie found a show that captured *Amma's* attention. The lecture on moral values and TV weddings stopped. Amma focused entirely on the show: a court show called *Judge For A Day*, currently ruling on a divorce case.

"What a deadbeat," Amma said. "Spending all his time playing *scramball*? I know Tyson hangs out in that bar a lot, but at least *he's* getting *viewing credits*. He's *watching* sports! That's honest work. Playing sports doesn't read in for anything at the end of the day. *Sports are for androids*."

The bell rang. This time, Boston didn't scurry past. Too absorbed in his new toys from Mr. Ology most likely.

"Two deliveries in one day?" Amma said. "I don't *think* so." Amma beat her foolish, little sister to the door. Sure enough, it was that wretched android delivery boy!

"Excuse me, Ma'am." The android craned his neck to peer around Amma. "I was hoping to speak with your sister. Lynnie?"

Lynnie shoved her way around her sister. "Hi. You came back..."

"Yeah, I was hoping..." The android knit and unknit the fingers of both hands. "I finished my shift for the day, and I was hoping to spend some time with you."

Lynnie blushed and smiled. "I'd like that."

Amma couldn't take it: "Unbelievable!"

Lynnie flashed her a frown and turned back to her android. "We could go back to my place. Watch *Symphony Wars* or *Rate That Jazz*..." The android looked disappointed. "Don't you like music? We could watch something else..."

"I don't get paid for watching," the android said. "The shows are made for you. I get paid for my delivery work. Anyway, I was thinking of something less...static."

Amma rolled her eyes. Leave it to an android to under appreciate their own creations.

He continued: "Perhaps a walk in the park?" Lynnie looked reluctant. "If you can't afford the time off, I can cover the difference in your viewing."

"That's sweet, but..."

Amma harrumphed, and said "Think what you'd be giving up?"

Lynnie looked at her infuriated sister and did exactly what she said: imagined what she *would* be giving up. An evening on the couch like every other, watching shows with her big sister.

Lynnie looked back at the man in front of her: he wasn't on

a show, picked specifically to suit her...but he was here, wanting to spend time with her. Were Tyson and Amma so perfect for each other? And how long would it be before she got on one of the shows anyway? If ever...

"I can afford it," Lynnie said. She held her hand out to her android and stepped outside.

Amma watched her little sister walk away. She *ought* to run after Lynnie, *save* Lynnie from herself, but... Well, an android in the family wouldn't be so bad. He'd have contacts, strings he could pull. Maybe, *just maybe*, she and Tyson, little Boston, and foolish Lynnie would all be starring on their own family drama come next Christmas.

Boston called his mother back inside, "Mum! *Wildertrek* is starting. You're *missing* it!"

6

WE CAN REMEMBER IT FOR YOU
RETAIL

Dylan reached into his pocket and pulled out his last *tenner*. He didn't especially feel like drinking coffee, but he thought it'd look strange if he didn't get something. Charlene ordered a double mocha frappacino and lemon cupcake with cream cheese icing. Dylan got the house coffee.

"Would you like to hear an advertisement?" a voice said in Dylan's ear as he and Charlene picked a table. He subvocalized, *yes*, and a catchy jingle for a laundromat down the street assaulted him. When the jingle finally ended, the voice in his head said, *"Six cents have been deposited in your account."*

He smiled, trying to cover his discomposure in front of Charlene, and asked, "What were you saying?"

"Trip Trapowski," she said. "He's so tortured as Douglas Quaid. I never realized he could act like that."

"Uh, yeah," Dylan said, completely stymied. He hadn't expected to be discussing acting and character after watching *Total Recall 3: Vacation on Jupiter*. Most of the comments he'd planned out during the movie had to do with the action sequences. In retrospect, that might not have been the brightest move. Nonetheless, Dylan tried gamely to engage Charlene's interest in "the particularly good bit with the amphibi-copter" or "that really neat looking time portal." Unfortunately, those conversation threads didn't last long, and soon they were back in unmapped waters.

"He was just so loyal to Melina. He looked at her like she was the only real thing in his whole world."

Dylan had to admit it was endearing that Charlene could turn a summer action flick into some kind of romance. "Well, they have quite a history from the other movies," he said, trying not to twitch as he listened to a LOL Burger ad in his head for the hundredth time this week. It ended as always with directions to the nearest *LOL Burger*, in this case, right across the street. The directions were kind of redundant with the giant billboard reading "Xtra Cheez? U Can Haz!" that Dylan could read through the coffee shop window.

Nonetheless, the ad gave Dylan the option of "continued, occasional, persuasive, visual advertising" as long as he was in the area. Dylan raised his coffee cup to cover his lips and accepted with trepidation, quickly reconfiguring his settings to allow visual ads. He usually turned offers like that down, preferring to keep his ears the portals of consumerism and his eyes pure. But, after this date with Charlene, he was going to be hurting for money.

"The thing I don't understand," Charlene said, looking pensive, "is why that old guy was so important. I mean, jeez, if I was Trip Trapowski, or Doug Quaid, or whatever, I wouldn't listen to some old geezer like that."

The words were out of Dylan's mouth before he could stop them: "What old guy?" Luckily, Charlene didn't seem to notice anything amiss, so maybe it wasn't so strange to not recognize the character from her description. Though, the girl who had just sat down at the table behind Charlene looked at Dylan askance.

"The doctor guy," Charlene explained. "The guy with those memory pills. The *old* guy."

"The guy with *Rekall, Inc*?" Dylan hazarded, thinking quickly.

"Uh... yeah..." Charlene answered. "I didn't get that at all. What was he all about?"

The girl at the other table shook her blue-haired head, but kept her eyes on the book she was reading. Dylan started to frown at her, wondering what she thought was so funny, but he quickly realized Charlene thought the look was meant for her. He flashed Charlene a smile, and her face melted into a smile back at him. Everything forgiven.

"I love going to see movies with you," Charlene said, reaching her hand across the table to hold his.

"Me too."

"Anyway," Charlene said, "What was I talking about? Oh, yeah. That old guy who Quaid was so freaked out by. What was up with that?"

Dylan said, "The first *Total Recall* started with Quaid getting memory implants at Rekall, Inc. So, we can't really be sure if all the stuff in the movies is real. Or just in Quaid's head." He hoped that was on the mark. And, if he was lucky, maybe the conversation would stay on the original movie now.

"There really was a first *Total Recall*?" Charlene asked. "I thought that starting off with number two last year was a joke. You know, 'cause there's time travel in it."

"Or like *Star Wars*," Dylan suggested.

"Huh?" Charlene asked, but Dylan was too busy puzzling over the weird look he was getting from the blue-haired girl to answer her. He wasn't used to getting looks like that from random girls in coffee shops. Fortunately, Charlene found herself at the end of her frappacino at just that moment. So, she missed Dylan's lack of attentiveness. "Hey, Dilly," she said, "I'm gonna get myself another drink. Kay?"

"Sure," Dylan said. "I'll be here."

Dylan watched Charlene walk back to the register, and once she was out of hearing range, he scooted his chair around the curve of the table, bringing him closer to the blue-haired girl. Keeping his voice low, he leaned over and asked her, "What's your problem? Huh? You keep giving me these weird looks."

The girl's mouth fell open, like she didn't know what to say. The silver piercing in her lip made a strange contrast to the blank innocence in her look of surprise. Dylan held her gaze, clearly expecting an actual answer. The girl pursed her pierced lips, pulled herself back together, and said, "You haven't seen *Total Recall 3*. Have you?"

"That's ridiculous," Dylan said. "My girlfriend and I just got back from seeing it in the theater."

The blue-haired girl pursed her lips again and the silver ring over the bottom one wiggled a little, like she was worrying it with her tongue while thinking. "Oh," she said. She looked toward the counter where Charlene was standing with a credit card, eyed her up and down, and then said, "I get it."

"What?" Dylan asked, annoyed—and a little afraid that this weird girl might actually have figured him out that fast. Then, seeing Charlene on her way back with a fresh frappacino and a second cupcake, he changed his tune to "*Never mind.*"

Blue-hair snorted and said, "No need to get defensive. Sheesh." But, to Dylan's relief, she turned back to her book after rolling her eyes at him. By the time Charlene sat herself down, their unwanted neighbor already had her nose buried deep in the time-worn pages.

"I bought you a cupcake," Charlene said. "I could see how you were eyeing mine." She placed a pale yellow morsel of baked goodness down on a plate before him. Dylan reached for the cupcake slowly, as if afraid it might run away if he reached too fast.

"The frosting is really good too," Charlene said, "but I

wasn't sure if you liked frosting. So, I figured plain was the safe bet." She shrugged.

"Thanks, Charlie," Dylan said, his mouth already full of moist but zesty, lemon cake. Her thoughtfulness almost drowned out the hit to his pride.

As they got back into discussing the movie, Dylan did most of the talking. He told Charlene all about the original. It was safer that way. Fewer ways to slip up. And, Charlene seemed genuinely interested. Besides, pedantically raving about obscure science-fiction came naturally to Dylan.

"You know," he said. "You can upload any movie from the 1900s for free. They run ad banners along the sides, but it's worth it. To watch all those great old movies."

"I'll have to look into that," Charlene said. "Maybe you can show me where you found them?"

While they talked, Dylan noticed a strange phenomenon. Stray cats had begun conglomerating in the coffee shop.

At first, it was just a grey tabby that snuck in at the feet of a customer. But, then there were several—orange and Jellicle—and, a few came trotting out from the kitchen. He wondered why no one shooed them away. Then, he wondered why no else seemed to notice them at all.

Then, a particularly plump orange-striped cat jumped up onto a nearby table, and opened its mouth wide in a giant caterwaul. Simultaneously, a vacant white space, like a hole in the fabric of reality, popped into place above it's head. Dylan was so surprised he jumped back, flinging out his arms and knocking over his chair in the process.

As he righted his chair, Dylan figured out what was going on. The white space was a cartoony speech bubble and it filled itself with the words: "I made u a cheezburger but I eated it!" It was like God opened a portal to him and typed out those words. Except, in this case, God was the LOL Burger corporation.

Dylan seated himself in his chair again, still surrounded by the spooky computer-virtual cats. They looked completely real until the speech and thought bubbles popped up over their heads. One by one, the cats "told" him things like "Goto LOL Burger *LOL!*" and "Yum xtra cheezy! LOL :-)" Then, one by one they filed away. Dylan closed his eyes and tried to rub the stain they'd left on his retinas away.

"You okay?" Charlene asked, probably for the third time. When Dylan dared open his eyes again, he saw that she looked worried and was mopping herself with napkins.

"Uh, yeah..." Dylan said, "I'm sorry..." He must have knocked Charlene's frappacino into her lap during his convulsions. "I got something in my eye," he said, cringing at the literal truth and simultaneous lameness of his excuse.

Charlene gave him an inquisitive look, but when he didn't say anything further she just shook her head and smiled. "If you're okay," she said, standing and looking about for the restroom. "I'm gonna get myself cleaned up, okay?"

"Sure," Dylan said, wondering if she knew about the *LOL cats* somehow. He'd tried to keep the blaring ads in his ears secret from her, but something about her look made him think she knew anyhow.

Besides, those cats were so vivid it was hard to believe anyone in the coffee shop *hadn't* seen them.

"Why don't you just tell her?" Blue-hair asked, clearly having waited until Charlene was safely away.

Dylan twisted around in his chair to look at the girl who kept bothering him. "Why are you eavesdropping on me?" he asked.

Blue-hair shrugged. "None of my friends wanted to see the new *Total Recall,*" she said. "So, I had no one to talk to about it. Besides, your girlfriend is cute."

Dylan couldn't tell if she meant it or was playing with him.

"Seriously," Blue-hair said. "You should tell her. I think she'd understand."

"What do you know?" Dylan said, more harshly than he meant. The stress of the evening was getting to him, and he was tired of playing his made-up part. "Her dad owns three LOL Burgers, and I couldn't even get a job at LOL Burger last summer." That wasn't entirely true, but it was close enough. The point was that Charlene had more money and fewer worries than him. It stung, and he'd been doing everything he could to hide his money-troubles from her. "If she knew I couldn't afford to take her to the movies and buy the rights to maintain the memories," his voice was losing its anger and taking on a tremulous edge, "...she'd dump me in a second."

"If you think that little of her," the blue-haired girl snapped back, "she should."

Dylan hadn't expected that. It surprised him enough that he really thought about it, and he was still thinking about it when Charlene returned. "Charlie," he said, "are you really interested in downloading old movies?"

"Yeah, sure." She was poking at her plate, scraping her nail on its surface. "I wonder what makes the plates here sparkly like that."

"Mineral dishwasher," Dylan answered, not thinking about the fact that Charlene would wonder how he knew. "After the wash-cycle, it sprays all the dishes with vitamin and mineral supplements."

From the way Charlene was looking at him, Dylan could tell she was putting the pieces together. He really needed to learn how to keep his mouth shut. Or maybe Blue-hair was right, and he shouldn't pre-judge Charlene for judging him. Either way, it was too late to keep this one in the bag.

"I worked the kitchens at Hot Diggity Dog last summer," he said.

Charlene smiled noncommittally. Maybe being honest with

her wouldn't be so bad. "So," she asked, "what movie should we go see next week?"

Dylan glanced behind Charlene and could see the blue-haired girl looking at him. Expectantly. He decided to take the plunge. "I can't really afford to go to a movie next week," he said. He couldn't see Charlene's reaction; he couldn't bring himself to look up at her. Instead, he fiddled with the healthily fortified plate in front of him.

When she didn't say anything, he forced himself to go on. "Actually, I couldn't really afford the movie tonight either. I..." He bit his lip, but he knew he had to say it. "I only had enough for the ticket in—I didn't pay for the memory-rights."

"What do you mean?" Charlene asked.

"They wiped the movie from my memory as soon as the credits were over. I don't actually remember anything other than sitting in the theatre next to you. Nothing on the screen."

"I didn't know you could do that," Charlene said.

She lived in such a different world. She'd never had to pinch pennies in her life.

"So..." Charlene said, dragging the syllable out, "when will you be able to afford to go see a movie again?"

"I don't think you understand," Dylan tried to say, but Charlene was still speaking: "Two weeks? 'Cause, we could do something different next weekend."

"Going out to the theater costs six times as much as downloading a movie at home, and...," he made a quick mental calculation, "...almost a hundred times as much as uploading the memory-rights direct."

Charlene was looking at him like, "*So?*"

Dylan opened his mouth to explain but found himself at a loss. He didn't know how to tell her that he'd only asked her to the movies in the first place to impress her. He hadn't expected it to become their weekly routine, and if he kept taking her to the theater, even without buying memory-rights, he wouldn't have enough money to make it through the rest of the semester. He'd already spent most of his savings from the summer at Hot Diggity Dog, and his scholarships barely covered room and board.

He knew he'd be working at Hot Diggity Dog again this summer, but he couldn't face the idea of going back to work before the end of the semester. When would he study? Between work and school, he wouldn't have time for Charlene then anyway.

That's what Dylan should have said, and maybe Charlene would have understood. But Dylan would have had to understand it himself to explain it, and all he knew was that thinking about Charlene and money made him feel bad. Inadequate. All he'd wanted was to talk to a girl about the coolness that was *Total Recall* and its sequels. Instead, he couldn't remember the third one, and the girl across from him had never heard of the first. It'd be another two weeks before he could afford the direct-to-brain upload rights... And he was more excited about that than kissing Charlene goodnight.

"This isn't working," Dylan said. "I don't think I can afford to go out with you."

"Afford?" Charlene asked, clearly affronted. But Dylan didn't know what to say to make it better. "I never expected you to spend money you couldn't. I never expected you to spend money on me at all."

Dylan started to point out that she'd expected to keep going to movies together, but he didn't think that would help. So, for the first time that evening, he kept his mouth shut.

"Would it help if I paid for the movie?" Charlene asked, but she could see Dylan bristle at the suggestion. "Okay... What if we... What if we just do stuff that's cheaper? Those old movies..."

Her voice was almost pleading now, and Dylan felt bad, knowing he was hurting her. He tried to picture hanging out in his dorm room watching old movies together, but it was too late. Something about the way she said "*old* movies," or maybe just the fact that looking at her made him feel even more inadequate now that he couldn't afford her or make her happy, pushed him over the edge. "I'm sorry," he said, and that was all.

Charlene pulled her jacket and bag off the back of her chair where they'd been hanging and put them on. She could tell it was over. They were over. But, before she left, she said, "Even if I couldn't remember the movie—if all I could remember was sitting next to you in the theater—I wouldn't want to give that up." She shrugged. "I guess you would."

Dylan watched Charlene walk out of the coffee shop. He wanted to comfort her; tell her she'd get over him; but, instead, he just let her go. The door swung shut behind her.

"Ouch," the blue-haired girl said, reminding Dylan she was there.

Dylan took a few moments to recover himself, then he said, "Well, that's what comes from following your advice." He meant it playfully—like the banter they'd had earlier—but, it may have sounded more like an accusation.

"You're better off," Blue-hair said. "A relationship built on mistrust and inequity is worse than no relationship at all."

"Uh, yeah," Dylan said, hoping she was right. "*Inequity*" and "*mistrust*" seemed like a bit of an exaggeration, but, it was true that he and Charlene hadn't had much in common. Though, she hadn't seemed to mind that.

"So," Dylan said, trying to keep the conversation going, tying to keep his mind off of the empty space that used to hold Charlene, "you've see the original *Total Recall*?"

"Sure," Blue-hair replied. "It's a classic."

"Much better than the sequel," Dylan added without even thinking about it.

Blue-hair smiled at him, and he felt a little better. She

wasn't like Charlene, but she was kind of cute. In an off-beat way. "What about *Star Wars*?" Dylan asked.

"Of course," she said. "I have a complete familiarity with pop culture from the 1900s through today."

"Huh?" Dylan asked, thinking that he might have more in common with this girl than he did with Charlene.

"It helps me relate to and understand clients," she said.

"Oh." Dylan wondered what it'd be like to kiss a girl with a pierced lip. And what other piercings she might have. "What kind of clients? What kind of work do you do?"

"I'm a counselor," Blue-hair said. "The free-trial version of *Emilia*."

Dylan let her comment sit for a moment, but it didn't sit well. "Free-trial version?" he asked.

"Yes. In our session tonight, I helped you locate a problem in your life and solve it."

Dylan felt a sinking feeling inside. He looked around the coffee shop, searching for a sane point of reference. Finally, he caught the eye of the girl at the counter. "Just a minute," he told Emilia, "I'll be back." Dylan's heart was pounding as he walked up to the coffee shop counter.

"Have you seen a blue-haired girl here tonight?" he asked the barista, almost whispering in his attempt to keep his voice down. Feeling crazy.

"Blue hair?" The barista said, louder than he liked, and laughed. "That went out of fashion, like, a century ago."

He looked back at Emilia, but she didn't look offended. "So...?"

"So, no."

Dylan stepped away from the counter feeling light-headed. He tried to remember when he'd first seen Emilia walk into the cupcake shop. He wasn't sure. He'd been paying all his attention to Charlene then.

"Is something wrong?" Emilia asked, looking worried, as

Dylan returned to his table. "I'm not authorized to help you with more than one problem per session."

Dylan stared at Emilia, and she looked completely real. As real as the table she was sitting at. As real as Charlene.

"If you found our session tonight helpful," Emilia said, flashing Dylan a smile that made him feel like tearing his eyes out, "you can sign up for the full version at an introductory price of just..."

But Dylan had stopped listening. He couldn't believe he'd broken up with Charlene on this advertisement's advice. He might as well rush off and buy a LOL burger every time he passed a billboard. Or every time he saw a cat...

"What am I going to do?" he said, putting his head in his hands. If Charlene were here, she'd take his hands in hers and tell him everything would be okay. Instead, Emilia told him, "I can't talk about that until you download the full version."

Dylan glared at her and tried to figure out how to undo the damage she'd done. If he participated in one of those psych studies, maybe it would pay enough to buy Charlene a dozen roses...

"Don't wait too long," Emilia said, rising from her chair and closing her book. "The current prices won't last." Then, before disappearing with an abruptness that left an orange after-image in Dylan's eyes, she added, "*Twenty-five cents have been deposited in your account.*"

7

———

THE OPPOSITE OF SUICIDE

Dennis took a bow and left the stage for his last time. He gripped arms with his brother and fellow band member; they grinned at each other and agreed it had been a good set. Cameras flashed, and fans shoved photos of him, hopefully, his way. He signed a few autographs, kissed a few girls, and made it to his car. This was the life. His job was being famous and adored, maybe singing a little too. When his day's work was done, he could head over to a party. There was always a party, every night. Tonight, the party was at the docks, on a house boat. It would be good, lots of new stuff to try... and Dennis tried it. The evening became swimmy before his eyes. The more stuff Dennis tried, the swimmier it became. Eventually, he started to feel like swimming. He remembered good old days, before everything got out of control. He used to go swimming then, just for fun. Now it was all commercial. The pressure was... so great. Maybe, if he could just go swimming again... just feel the water passing by him... flowing...

Dennis found himself standing by the edge of the boat, looking at the water. It shone, not with reflected light, but with its own spiritual light from within. Spirituality, that's what they'd lost. If he could just go swimming, maybe he'd find it again. Dennis stepped over the railing, and, leaning into the cold, night air, he called back to his friends. "I'm looking for something I lost..." He jumped before they could respond.

The plunge took Dennis deep into the icy water. Dark, cold, and wet enfolded him, enclosed him, and promised to never let him go. A last gulp, and not a gulp of air. Dennis died.

Or did he? The cold and wet that held him so firmly began to recede. Dennis felt himself standing on his feet. His mind felt strange. His back was warm... his body felt strange. Memories started to return to him, but they were not memories of his life as Dennis. They were longer, older memories. Dennis felt like a moviegoer, sitting in a theater, when the lights come up. It was like the moment when, suddenly, you're no longer Marlon Brando in *On The Waterfront*; you're just you. But who was Dennis?

Remembering himself, the creature who had so recently been Dennis sighed. He felt old. His was too long a life. To die like Dennis had... Like he had, just a moment ago, when he was Dennis... If only it would stick. He could die a million times, as a million different people, and every time he would come back. Such was the curse of being a Sheltorianack.

Dennis, or rather the Sheltorianack who had recently been Dennis but had now returned to being Csive, opened his eyes to the devastatingly familiar sight of The Arcade. The game before him, the one that let him live the life of Dennis, was flashing its lights, telling him that he'd died and the game was done. A Sheltorianack behind him, growing impatient, tapped him on the shoulder. "If you're done, buddy," it growled, "then move along."

Csive turned his ancient self around. The line behind him was long. He remembered standing in line a thousand times for a thousand years each time to be Dennis. It was one of the popular games, although not nearly as popular as John

Lennon. Glamour. Rock stars. Those kinds of games were popular. In fact, they were second only to great political leaders. Csive remembered being Napoleon a few eons back. He'd liked Joan of Arc better. He played at being her at least a trillion times in a row once. Right now, he couldn't quite remember why... It was an awfully long line for such a short, piously tame life. It must have been one of his moods.

For members of an immortal race, moods last a very long time. They come and go, and most Sheltorianacks have gone through all flavors of them more than several times. The stripy, green and purple fellow behind Csive, the impatient one, was clearly going through a particularly flamboyant phase. He was rude, impatient, and reactive. He'd decked himself out with bangly bracelets and loud clothes, mostly in hideous oranges. It would get him nowhere. In a couple millennia he would tire of it. Perhaps then he would become depressed and reflective like Csive. Until then, Csive figured, it was probably better to keep out of his way, so Csive excused himself from the front of the line. With a grunt of satisfaction, the impatient and gaudily dressed Sheltorianack moved into place and dropped his token in the arcade machine.

Csive wandered around the glaring halls of The Arcade aimlessly. He considered leaving the human section, going to a section with games from a different universe. He could play Grangledor of Azton IV again. That was a particularly fun life. Except, Csive just didn't care enough. This was a bad phase he was in. He didn't remember ever feeling so low before, so much as if life, all life, was pointless. But, he'd lived such a very long time, he probably had felt this way many times before. He'd probably even felt worse. He couldn't even revel in his depths of depression being novel or new.

Eventually Csive, unable to muster the enthusiasm necessary to stay standing in a line long enough to get to the front of it, ended up playing a game he found tucked away in the corner without any line. Csive dropped a token in the machine and felt his memories drain out of him. He did like that feeling. It made the monotony of infinity briefly disappear. A moment later, in Sheltorianack time, Csive returned to being himself, much as he had after being Dennis. He remembered playing this game before: Jim Tyson was an accountant, who was teased a lot during his early childhood, never knew how to talk to girls, lived sixty-three years without ever marrying, and died in his bed from heart failure. It was a boring life; it was a boring game. Csive dropped another token in to play a couple more thousand times before he couldn't take that particular brand of boredom anymore.

After wandering among the games a few eons longer, including a break where Csive chose to stand on one foot as long as could, which turned out to be a rather long time, Csive happened on the arcade game that's you. Csive dropped a toekn in, and he was born as you, lived your life, and died. He returned to being Csive. That was a pretty good game, he thought. Immediately afterwards, the thought depressed him. He would have played the game again, but he couldn't stand the idea of being you again, knowing he'd only return to being himself afterwards. Besides, he'd played every game in The Arcade an uncountable number of times before. Csive left The Arcade and went home.

On the way home, Csive was struck by a horrible, terrible, morbidly fascinating idea. He couldn't, despite many attempts, get it out of his head. It was the first new idea he'd had in... well, more years than you and all the people you've ever known have lived, all put together and multiplied by the number of carbon atoms in all of your bodies. To think of a new idea... the wonder, the happiness! But it was a horrible idea, Csive reminded himself, and it could only bring him pain. But... it was *new*.

Csive, in spite of himself, found himself building a new

arcade game to test his idea. It was an arcade game like no other, the first of it's kind. A small voice, the voice of reason, a voice little listened to when in the throws of a deep depression, suggested to Csive that hopefully this machine would not only be the first but also the last of its kind. In fact, the tiny, beleaguered voice suggested, maybe it shouldn't even be the first...

Csive, in a passion, didn't listen. Novelty was all he had to live for at the moment, and since his immortality left him no choice but to live, he was left with little choice but to pursue the dangerous novelty.

Finally, the new game machine was done. It stood before Csive, flashing its displays, blinking its lights, enticing him to play. It would be stupid... beyond stupid... more impossibly horrible than anything that any of the people he'd ever been could imagine... to play such a game. Their lives were too small to allow comprehension of such a horror.

Csive stood before the machine for minutes, hours, days, years, eons... a time as long as our universe has existed and longer. He couldn't care about anything enough to convince himself to take one step away from the machine. He dropped a token in.

Csive began his own, immortally long and now fractally longer, life again.

8

———

SMALL SMOOTH PEBBLE

Jenny felt inside her pocket. There was a small, smooth pebble that she'd been hiding since she was tiny. A multi-dimensional creature had appeared to her and begged her to keep it safe. If she dug her fingernail into it...

But she mustn't. She mustn't. She had to be strong.

See, it was the self-destruct button for the universe.

And... She knew she shouldn't use it.

She shouldn't.

But she dug her fingernail in anyway.

And everything was over. Forever.

9

ON THE EVE OF THE APOCALYPSE

Dear Patriarchal Genetic Progenitor,

In spite of my requests that you leave me alone, I find notifications and messages from you, little traces of your electronic existence, in every aspect of the virtual world whenever I dare to tread in it. Generally, I ignore your unwanted advances toward a relationship that I gave up long ago. But tonight, knowing that the Elasporians will descend to Earth tomorrow, I find that the idea of reaching out to you and your myriad tiny abuses is less painful and frightening than the reality that all flesh-bodied humans will face tomorrow.

So I'm writing you this missive. You're probably reading it as I write, your electronically quickened mind now able to flit from one corner of the net to the other faster than I can blink one of my mundanely physical eyes. I know—you think I should upload my mind to the net too. You probably think you were being generous in offering to pay for it. But I don't want your money. I don't want to be uploaded. You never have respected my choices or beliefs—the way that I feel my physical body is a true and necessary part of who I am.

I know that you claim you didn't vote in favor of the Elasporians' imminent occupation of Earth. But you couldn't have fought very hard against it. You and your uploaded cronies have nothing to lose when the sinuous snake-like reptiles from Antares come to wrap their venom-oozing bodies around the fleshy humans left on Earth, digesting and dissolving us from the outside in. It will be horrific. But you won't have to see it—you can level a new warlock class character in World of Life-craft to 60 and simultaneously read the epic poems of Davi D., the new avant-garde AI, all while composing your own memoir about how your daughter wronged you by being too stubborn to give up her body and become code floating through the computers of the world.

I would unplug those computers if I could. Don't doubt that. If the great halls where the computers are housed weren't surrounded by killer robots, I wouldn't be the only one. We'd come to unplug them en masse—all our fleshy hands pawing obscenely at the electronic veins of your mechanical hearts and brains.

But tomorrow, I'll watch my fleshy friends, one by one, be captured and eaten as delicacies by space snakes that you invited here, because they could make your computer world run a little faster. Technicians, who only asked that you let them eat the vestigial physical bodies you'd left behind. Even if some of them hadn't been left behind—some of those bodies still have people inside them. Like me.

I don't expect to live long once the Elasporians descend from the metal space saucers, so this will likely be our last communication. I have to admit, you taught me three things before you abandoned me for your virtual world.

1. How to peel a grapefruit properly, removing all the bitter membranes and leaving only the sweet.

2. And this one's really ironic—some excellent video game strategies, back when you were a real person in a real physical body. I guess, for you now, those video game strategies would

count as actual life lessons. Your entire life is a video game. But not for me. For me, it was a way to while away a few useless hours.

3. How it feels to be disrespected—and as a consequence, to never allow anyone to disrespect me.

So thank you for those lessons. I don't think the first two will serve much of a purpose any longer. But as the Elasporian venom melts my flesh tomorrow, I will hate the insidious space snake that's eating me alive with every fiber of my being—every fiber of my hatred for you.

Goodbye Father.

10

MY MAGIC, MY SPELL

You stole a piece of my power from me. And it took me fifteen years to recognize it.

We were acolytes together, studying under Mage Dawlins. I studied ice magic. You studied fire. And Tilly was studying flora spells. She is part of this. She always was. We both loved her. No, I'm giving you too much credit. I make that mistake. I've been making it for years. It's a hard habit to kill.

I loved Tilly—her impish smile; the subtle, clever jokes she told that wouldn't fully hit me until hours later; and of course, the way she could summon flowers from the cracks in the concrete and paint murals on the walls in shades of moss before she'd ever been formally taught the spells. Life magic flowed through her. And she glowed with delight at every new spell she learned.

I loved her. You dated her.

Her long dark hair would fall in front of her face when she leaned over her spell books, too focused on her studies to notice, and you could sweep it away from her face, tuck it behind an ear, playfully touching her cheek, her chin, and finally distracting her completely with a kiss. I only watched, trying not to care. I didn't have time for romance anyway. Ice magic is a slower magic than others. Powerful, yes. But only after years of study. Life magic produces a veritable fireworks display of brightly colored petals even in the hands of the newest initiates. Fire magic is more flashy still. But ice? It takes time. Time to control. Time to appreciate. Time to develop into the powers I have now.

I can create castles of ice on the surface of a sun-beaten pond in midsummer. I can draw water from the air and fill a room with sparkling chandeliers, carefully crafted prisms that cast rainbows from their facets.

But I couldn't back then. All I could do was make an ice cube form—perfectly square in every dimension—in the middle of a beaker of room temperature water. Mage Dawlins was impressed. She encouraged me. She knew it was hard watching her other acolytes show off their dancing flowers and swirling flames while all I had to show for my work was a lump of inanimate ice. If I focused really hard, I could make it wibble wobble in its tepid bath, spreading ripples over the surface of the water in the beaker.

Then one night when we sneaked into Dawlins private library—you, me, and Tilly—we found a book with arcane spells, magic that didn't fit into the primary fields of study. We weren't supposed to be there, and Tilly kept giggling, excited, maybe scared we'd be caught. The fear—just a little, not too much, because what would Dawlins really do to us?—made it more fun. We each picked a spell and copied it down, planning to learn them later. Tilly picked a spell for tantalizing squirrels, making them into temporary minions. I didn't pay enough attention to yours, but I know now what it was. I recognize it whenever I read the papers lately. All of the stories... All of the mages hurt... All of the power stolen. I am ahead of myself. We'll get there.

I picked a simple memory spell, a forgetting spell. I wanted to forget the fool I'd made of myself in mundane school before I knew I was a wizard, before I knew about wizards at all. I wanted to forget the fight I'd had with my mother, the horrible things I'd said to her before leaving to be apprenticed to Mage Dawlins. It was a foolish wish, a young, naive wish. But I was young and naive, and it was late at night. I was giggling with friends, and it all seemed so fun.

So I copied the spell down, and I studied it. I stayed in the library all night. At some point, Tilly left, hoping to find a squirrel in the trees on the school grounds to make dance with her new skills. You left with her. You always followed her lead. I stayed studying, because I studied more slowly. I always struggled to learn what came easily to the rest of the acolytes. But I was not going to be foiled. I was not going to miss out on my part of the fun, just because I couldn't learn as fast.

I fell asleep. I thought I was safe. I was in my teacher's personal library. I was seventeen, and no one had ever touched me without my permission before. I had shared spells with a boy once—holding out our hands palm to palm, letting my ice magic flow into him and his earth magic flow into me. With our hands together, he had cooled his drink at the dining hall table, and I had cracked one of the clay plates. He'd laughed and I'd smiled. It was beautiful, consensual, completely shared and completely under my control.

But what happened to me that night was not.

I woke up, head against the hard wood of the desk I'd been studying at and arms tingling from the edge of the table cutting off their circulation. But my shoulder—bare because it had been an unseasonably warm spring, and I was wearing a sundress—tingled too. I felt your hand against my shoulder, and I looked up surprised. Did you want something? I would have asked, but instead I felt the magic flowing out of me. No magic returned. Just leaving, flowing from my shoulder into the hot skin of your hand.

"There's no time," you said. "Tilly will be in trouble for using the squirrel spell if I don't get to Dawlins and use the forgetting spell you've been studying right away."

"Okay," I mouthed, unable to fully summon my voice. You knew how to manipulate me. How to convince me I would have okayed your actions if you'd only asked, convince me that I'd given you tacit permission through my unspoken love for Tilly. But you didn't ask. I didn't give permission. You pulled the spell straight out of my body, and then you used the spell you'd learned earlier that night—the one that would let you keep it.

I fell back asleep feeling dirty, feeling drained. When I woke up again, I convinced myself I could never have learned such a difficult spell as the forgetting spell. It must have been a dream. If I had learned the spell, I would have still known it. Wouldn't I? Spells can only be borrowed, not stolen. As far as I knew. I wasn't sure what had happened, and when I asked Tilly about that night, her face flushed red, and her tongue stumbled, more embarrassed and flustered than I'd ever seen her before. But one thing was certain—she couldn't make squirrels dance. She wouldn't even look at squirrels anymore.

But sometimes, when you walked under the trees, the branches above rustled and swayed. I swear, some days the squirrels waltzed when you walked past.

After that night, Mage Dawlins kept her private library locked. Tilly broke up with you, quit her studies, and moved away, back to being mundane. (I know she gave up magic, but I hope she at least gardens. I hope there are still flowers in her life.) And I focused on my studies, pushing my feelings for Tilly away deep inside. I might have reached out to her, continued our friendship at least, but I could no longer think about her without my feelings being tainted by thoughts of you.

I was in awe of you, such a powerful magician. I followed you around, studying near you, wishing a piece of your greatness would rub off on me. What I really wanted was my own magic back, the piece of my life—no matter how small—that you had stolen. But I couldn't see that. All I could see was your allure. Your magic. Your power.

You had to be powerful. I could never have turned a piece of my own magic over to you permanently, so if it wasn't a dream, you had to have learned the spell on your own, glancing over my shoulder, reading a spell one time through that I had been studying uselessly all night, too dense to understand. But that's not what happened. It's what I believed for many years, but it's not true. You took my spell from me, leaving me to doubt myself, second guess every spell I learned after that one, always wondering if I was good enough or if somehow my magic would inexplicably slip away, leaving me less than I had been before I started. And I wasn't the only one you did this to.

You grew more and more powerful. So did I. But not as fast as you. None of us grew as fast and as powerful as you, because you no longer needed to study. Only to touch—take the spells; erase the taking. You've been doing it for years, building an empire of every flavor and color of magic, all stolen.

But you've finally been caught, and mages across the land are beginning to remember the power you've taken from them. They're coming to recover their spells, and your fireballs—the only spell that was ever truly yours, or did you steal that one somehow too?—cannot keep them all away.

You are not magical. You never were. You are a thief.

You are nothing.

And I am stronger with my ice powers than you will ever be. I can build a carapace of ice for myself, armor that chills the air around me and protects me from your fireballs. I can skate on blades of ice across frost rivers that form at my command, personal highways arching and flowing like ribbons through the air. I can throw blades of ice, thinner than leaves and sharper than knives that shatter into shrapnel as bright and pointed as needles, only to melt away after their damage is done.

You will not be able to stop me. You haven't been able to stop the others. You are losing already.

As more and more of your memory spells wear off with the crumbling passage of time, more and more of us will come to take our power, our spells back, until every last breath of your stolen magic is gone. You will be left with nothing but a memory that you cannot erase.

Because that spell is mine.

11

ANGER IS A PORCUPINE, SADNESS IS A FISH

The child with a malformed arm, bent like a bird's folded wing, had passed through Troway Village a year ago. Now Dara was a traveler like he had been. Would her old village welcome her? A prodigal daughter returned? Or would she be hurried along like the child and his parents had been?

Dara and Iassandra had been the town's truth-tellers together back then. When the villagers had come to them, not knowing what to think of the strange child traveling through their village, Dara had sung a song of gods' blessings, how they bent the unborn child's arm, marking him and setting him apart as he grew. She sang that he should be welcomed and taken in, a child touched by a god.

Iassandra had sung of illness, deterioration, and decay. The villagers had believed her; the child with his god-touched wing had barely made it out of town alive. Dara had left shortly afterward, unable to stay in a town owned by a poisonous tongue.

After a year of travels, the dusty streets of Dara's home were the same, so familiar as to make Dara's heart clench inside her. She hadn't known how much she missed her home until she returned. She passed Corin selling fresh bread, and he smiled at her. Children ran through the streets, bumped into her, and flashed her friendly smiles too. She recognized the children's faces, but they were longer, thinner, older than they had been. Closer to adults.

At the town square, a crowd gathered, listening to a voice Dara couldn't make out. She came closer, listening to hear the news, hoping it was good, but all she could make out, floating above the crowd's heads, was a hissing, whispering sound. Dara pressed her way into the crowd, working her way between old friends who exclaimed with delight at seeing her before turning back, hushedly, to listen to the hissing sounds.

Dara couldn't understand the words, but she felt her skin prickling at their sound; it had to be Iassandra, singing a song of Dara's return. The formerly friendly faces around Dara grew impassive, and Dara felt her own face grow numb and strange. Her back arched, and the people around her moved aside, leaving a space surrounding her, an empty bubble, as if her body were covered in a porcupine's sharp quills, keeping the people away.

Dara remembered the child with his wing-like arm and how her own song had told him that he would fly some day. His eyes had shone while she sung. Then Iassandra had sung, and his arm had become a poisonous serpent, eating away at him. He would never fly.

A year later, Iassandra was still singing, and the whole town listened to her.

If Dara was filled with anger, it was earned. Her face protruded into a muzzle, and she spat her anger at the dusty ground. She would own the porcupine quills growing from her back, bending her into a chimera of rage.

Corin with a loaf of fresh bread tucked under his arm approached Dara tentatively. He held the bread forth and said, "I'm so sorry. But you should go. Take this bread for the road."

Suddenly, Dara's rage washed away, knocking her from her feet. The quills sank into her back, flattening against her and widening into slippery scales. She flopped to the ground, sadness filling her like a gasping fish. She had only just returned home. How could she lose it again? Must she travel for another year? And another? Would she ever come home again?

Corin placed the bread beside her and backed away, not looking at the useless incarnation of sadness she had become. Her mouth opened and closed, voicelessly calling her pain.

The crowd started to clear, and Dara looked up to see Iassandra, still singing her song, but Dara didn't see the same small woman that all the others saw.

Dara saw the creature that she had cursed her former friend to be—in Dara's eyes, Iassandra's face was framed by the hissing, fork-tongued mouths of a dozen snakes. If Iassandra's words could change Dara into a porcupine of anger, a fish of sadness, then Dara would cast her own spell of words.

Finding her voice, her singing, truth-telling voice, for the first time in a year, she yelled, "You Gorgon!" She yelled it loud; she yelled it clear. The words escaped her mouth moments before her lips hardened, turning to stone.

But as the crowd heard Dara's words, as the spell of her voice sank into them, each member of the crowd turned to see their town truth-teller, Iassandra, in the light of Dara's curse.

Snake-faces hissed, trying to weave their spell, but Iassandra's words had lost their power. All she could do was freeze her audience with her own impotent rage.

Stone spread through the crowd, faces hardening, eyes glinting like black marble, all of them staring at the gorgon in their midst. All of them turned to stone, except Iassandra.

Alone in the midst of statues, Iassandra's snake-faces snarled and rasped, spewing their poison, but no one heard.

12

RETURNING THE LYRE

The snake didn't bite me. It bit Orpheus, and his lyre twanged discordantly as he fell to the ground. It was the first inharmonious sound that perfect instrument had ever made. It was the sound that started my journey. It was a claw, hooked inside my ear, ripping and tearing away every illusion I'd had of safety and happiness, shattering my dreams of a future with Orpheus.

Apollo, my father-in-law, came to the funeral, stood beside the pyre with me, and watched his son—my beloved—shed his mortal coil, that alabaster skin, and rise as smoke into the sky. The fire roared, but the smoke that had been Orpheus made no sound.

When the embers were cold and the guests dispersed, I still wept beside the burned out pyre. Apollo brought me his son's lyre. "Keep this," the god said, radiance shining from his hair, his eyes. "It should be yours."

I looked at the lyre in my hands. It had no meaning without Orpheus's fingers to pluck it. I looked up, prepared to offer the gift back to this god who was no longer truly my kin, but Apollo the man was gone. Instead there was a fleecy white cloud in the sky, sunlight beaming from behind, outlining it in silver. If I shouted to the cloud, "Take it back! I don't want it!", would the god who'd been beside me only a moment before hear me? Or would I be mad? A girl lost in grief, screaming at the sky?

Other than the cloud, the sky was clear. There was already no sign of the plain gray smoke that had been my Orpheus. He'd gone to Hades.

Grief is strange. As it grabs your throat and strangles you, you think you couldn't possibly hurt any more; then it finds a way to punch your guts, doubling you over in pain deeper still. My Orpheus had no lyre with him in Hades' realm.

Those perfect fingers had no strings to pluck. I would never hear his music again either way, yet it was infinitely worse to know that his music wasn't happening at all, not even damp-ened by the sadness dripping from the cave walls in the Underworld.

The lyre in my hands should have been burned in the pyre. I shoved it into the ashy rubble, but there was no heat left to burn it and carry it to Orpheus in smoke across the sky.

I would have to take it to him myself.

How do you pack for a trip into the Underworld? Dress warmly? As if any layer of wool could cut the cold of death. Or shield me from the molten fires of the river Phlegethon.

I wandered the small house Orpheus and I had shared, picking up cooking utensils, putting them down, considering light shawls and thick bulky blankets. Eventually, I took none of it. I walked out of my house, wearing my best shoes and holding his lyre against my heart. The gods would smile on my quest, or I would die in the woods, searching for the rent in the Earth where the river Styx flows down to Hades' realm.

~

I COULD TELL you about the months I spent wandering, eating unripe berries and wondering why I didn't starve; the days I spent stumbling through the dark caverns once I found the way down; the three-headed hell-hound who sniffed Orpheus's lyre with three wet noses, whimpered, and looked away; and the Ferryman who made lewd jokes about the living girl—until he saw the lyre. Once Charon knew I was Orpheus's—the wife of a god, even a demi-god, even a dead one—his tongue grew still.

I could tell you about these things—how the waters of the river Styx lapped at the sides of the ferry, how I saw my reflection in that dark mirror and watched myself age and youthen erratically on the water's surface. When I saw my smooth face lined with wrinkles, my gold hair turned white, I wondered what life that woman had lived. Had she remarried and borne children for a human husband? Or had she been too hooked on the drug of godhood and devoted herself to the study of Athena's arts? Perhaps she had become a great weaver with fingers like spider legs, spindly yet soaked in talent, pickled with carefully developed skill.

I smiled at my older self; instead of smiling back, her years and lines faded away into the shallow beauty and pure joy of childhood. She became a girl who had not yet heard plinking strains of music rise from a fireside to wind around her heart.

I could tell you all these things. I could.

But the memory of them is swallowed up in the retelling. They become stories instead of breathless moments, clung to by a mind still sorting itself out.

I defined my life when, after all my journeying, I stood before Hades—not only a god but also a king—and asked him to guide me to Orpheus, to let me return his lyre, and bring music to the Underworld.

Persephone's eyes caught mine; she leaned over and whispered in her husband's ear. Then the king of the Underworld proclaimed: "You cannot go to Orpheus." He offered me a choice instead.

I could give the lyre to Hades, who would hand it along to his great-grandson, or I could turn around, leave the Underworld carrying the lyre, never once looking back, and Hades promised that Orpheus would follow me home. I had to make it all the way to our small house, without once looking over my shoulder or turning back, and Orpheus would walk through the threshold with me, safely mine again once we were inside.

Hades promised.

But all the gods are tricksters, even the dour king of the Underworld.

I looked to Persephone, the stolen woman, trying to read her expression, wondering what she had whispered and wishing she could advise me, but she gazed into the distance, no longer looking at me.

As I weighed my options, feeling the heavy impatience of Hades' stone-eyed gaze, I realized that if it was a trick, the harm was already done. My heart kept leaping inside of me, practicing the moment of joy I already expected. Over and over again, I pictured myself reaching home, turning around, and seeing Orpheus. My heart rehearsed the happiness I would feel, as if it could beat hard enough to jump past the hours and days of walking, wondering whether I'd been made a fool and would once again face the heartbreak of losing my love.

My heart had heard Hades' offer and accepted it; my head had no say.

WITH EVERY STEP AWAY FROM HADES' throne room, I listened to hear footsteps join me from behind but heard only echoes of my own. Or were they echoes? Maybe I could hear Orpheus. Maybe my love was following, only a few paces behind. I held that hope tightly, imagining I could feel his breath in the air between us, binding us together, all through Hades' kingdom. I had faith.

Until I saw the fear in Charon's eyes.

The Ferryman looked at me nervously. He had not expected my return. "This is unnatural," he muttered, but he let me in the boat.

The ferry rocked on the water, disturbed by my weight. I stepped forward and seated myself on the bench in the front, leaving room on the back bench for Orpheus. The boat rocked again, but Charon had plunged his oar into the water. I couldn't be sure if there were two or three of us in the ferry.

All the way across, Charon didn't speak to me or meet my eye. Instead, he kept looking past me, possibly watching Orpheus, possibly staring aimlessly into the distance. I couldn't tell. I could tell that he was afraid. Was it because I'd transgressed the natural barriers of the world, descending into the Underworld and returning... alone? Was it because Orpheus had transgressed those barriers, and was sitting in the boat behind me?

Or was it something worse?

~

THIS IS A STORY OF DOUBTS. A story of continuing on, in spite of them.

~

A STORY of those doubts plaguing you.

~

By the far side of the River Styx, I was convinced that Hades had sent not Orpheus to follow me, but instead a demon who would follow me home and destroy my village as punishment for my impudence and hubris. Everyone I knew would suffer, and it would be my fault.

Yet, even then, I didn't look over my shoulder. I hoped too fiercely that Orpheus was following me. I would risk everything —not only my own life, but also the lives of others who I had no claim to—to get my Orpheus back.

As I reentered the world of the living, I wished I had asked Charon who was in the boat behind me. I wished I had looked down into the water; perhaps, I could have seen Orpheus's reflection and known for sure. Of course, I had done neither of these things, because I was afraid they'd be cheating. I was afraid I'd see Orpheus's face on the water, and he'd melt away, exactly as Hades had promised he would. I was afraid Charon would laugh at me, taunt me, and tell me made-up details of the demon in Orpheus's place such that I couldn't resist looking back at him. And he would melt away.

All my fears were wrapped up in that phrase: melt away.

Yet as I wandered, seemingly alone, through the forests that had brought me to the Underworld in the first place, the pressure built inside me. Every moment, I fought the desire to glance over my shoulder. It was an ache, an itch, an urge that was always with me. I had to know if he was there.

So, I took a risk and started singing a song that I always got wrong. I could never quite remember the lyrics to it or hit the notes right. When Orpheus was alive, all I had to do was start singing, and he would take over.

But his voice didn't rise from behind me. I brushed my fingers over the strings of his lyre, hoping to hear him reprimand me and tell the story of how Hephaestus had forged the gold frame; Hermes had sacrificed five perfectly snow-white lambs to provide the strings; and Apollo had gifted the finished lyre to him for his tenth birthday.

Yet although the lyre twanged discordantly under my clumsy fingers, Orpheus did not object.

All is well, I told myself, relieved somehow by the mere act of singing. Hades would not allow Orpheus to speak before we reached home. That was all. A spell of silence.

As the days passed, though, my doubts grew stronger. At times, I was sure that I was walking through the forests alone. I awoke every morning from nightmares of Orpheus, smiling at me, kissing me, and then melting away like mist. I lived in fear of forgetting myself for even a single moment and looking over my shoulder.

All day as I walked, my mind focused on controlling my eyes, keeping my gaze straight ahead, but my heart practiced the disappointment I would feel when I arrived home to find Orpheus had never been behind me, alternated with practicing the joy I would feel when I saw him again. The feelings were more tiring than the miles of walking.

By the time our small house was in sight, I was almost too afraid to enter it.

DID I LOOK BACK? All the way through my story, that has been the question. If I had known the answer before I started, how much suffering could have been saved? At times, it felt like the uncertainty itself would kill me.

I CROSSED the threshold of our house, and on the other side, I closed my eyes. I stood there frozen, unable to look, afraid I wouldn't see Orpheus, afraid I'd misremembered Hades'

command, missed some arcane requirement, and I would see Orpheus but only for a moment, only for the last time.

I felt the lyre lifted from my hands and then warm lips on my cheek. "Open your eyes, my love, my savior, my Eurydice."

He was there, and I felt all the joy in the world.

I was never happier to see anyone than to see Orpheus when I opened my eyes. His regal mouth tilted in a charmingly crooked smile that took my breath away, and his deep brown eyes sparkled with love that I felt mirrored in my own.

Orpheus's perfect fingers played the lyre I returned to him, moving with a deft dexterity that I knew would play upon my own body soon, and strains of music bent the universe around us into pure beauty. He improvised a song for me of our voyage together that felt more real than the endless voyage had itself. I could hardly tell the difference between real life and a dream, because my life had become the moment I'd dreamed of for so long.

BUT IT DIDN'T LAST. Life moved on and became normal again. I miss that moment.

AND NOW I WONDER.

I catch myself, looking away when I hear his voice, afraid that if I see him, he'll disappear, forgetting that Hades' curse hangs over us no longer.

And I wonder about the lives I imagined. The child growing in my belly now, conceived the night we made it home from the Underworld, will be a demi-god like his father. Gods cause trouble, and I'm afraid of what our child will be. How much easier would it be to raise a fully human child? Or to have devoted myself to Athena, and not have a child at all?

Somehow, I never noticed the way that Orpheus flirted with the nymphs and naiads before. I felt so lucky simply for him having picked me. Now I've earned his love. I rescued him from death, and I feel he owes me better than singing love songs to every pretty girl and boy who swoons at the demi-god's feet.

Those months of never looking over my shoulder took a toll. I wouldn't change my choice, but before Hades forced me to make a choice, and remake it over and over for months on end, I loved Orpheus simply with my whole heart.

Now I wonder, who would I have become if I'd let him melt away? Would I like myself better? Would my life be easier?

Could I have fallen in love again with a man whose face didn't make me want to close my eyes?

When will my doubts melt away?

When will I recover from returning that lyre?

13

THE FISH KITE

Joan opened the door to see her ex-fiancé slumped against the door frame. Leland was a lion of a man. Tall, blonde, preternaturally confident. She'd only seen him looking haggard and haunted like this once before, ten years ago, when his memory drugs had worn off. That had been the beginning of their end.

"Come inside," she said.

Leland followed her like a lamb through the apartment, stepping carefully around piles of toys that Joan's daughter hadn't put away. Kayla was at kindergarten. Joan had an hour before she had to go pick up the five-year-old. Taping together an old ex wasn't what she wanted to do with the time, but she'd known this was coming. Ever since Leland had lost the election for governor.

Joan fixed tea for both of them, and they sat down at the kitchen table. She placed her hand on the book she wasn't reading.

Leland stared at his tea. He didn't say anything.

"How much do you remember?" Joan asked. He was clearly off of his memory drugs again.

"Everything," Leland said.

Just like last time. The idea of it hit her in a wave, crashing down, fanning out, seeping into the sand of her being. It had been easy to move on from Leland, because once he wiped his memory clean of her, it was like the man she loved no longer existed. Except in her own memories. But if he remembered— all the time they'd spent together, all the in-jokes, all the suffering after their friend Michael had died... Leland was back for real. This was her Leland. She'd been married for eight years, most of them happy, to Andrew. She didn't want Leland back, but part of her soul reached out, desperate to reconnect with the person she'd lost.

But it wouldn't last.

"So, what is this?" Joan asked. "Some sort of second good-bye? Closure before you start taking the drugs again?"

"I'm not taking them."

Joan wanted to argue with him. To say, "For now." She wanted to believe that if he'd abandoned his memories with her that he was a man who'd always abandon his memories. A man defined by abandonment. But there was no room in his mood, his posture, his tone to question his words. He meant them. "Why this time?"

Leland looked up from his untouched tea. The sparkle that had always characterized his eyes had become a hard glint. His entire demeanor had taken on an edgy, soulful quality that he'd never had with her. It's hard to be edgy or soulful when you've never experienced the slightest hardship. At least, not that you can remember. He'd always erased the slighted pain, so as far as he knew, he'd lived a golden life.

"Why do you think?" he asked.

Joan frowned. She'd never understood him taking the memory drugs in the first place. Why would she know why he'd quit?

"If I forget that I lost the election... If I forget that I ever ran...

I'll want to run again." He sounded angry, frustrated. Either with himself or the world. Probably both.

"Right," Joan said.

He'd be stuck in a loop. Everyone knew about his memory drug addiction now. It had been all over the news. His campaign managers hadn't known to hide it, because Leland hadn't warned them. He hadn't remembered it himself. He never did, until something went wrong. Then the floodgates opened, and he remembered every failure he'd erased from his life, every moment of pain. Each painful memory reminding him of the next in a long chain.

Joan remembered finding Leland on the floor after Michael's death, sobbing over an orange bottle of pills, blubbering about the tiniest slights and insults from his early childhood. Especially a fish kite that he'd spent hours making as a child. He had made her look for that fish kite with him in his mother's attic over and over again, convinced that it must be carefully saved somewhere. Yet they could never find it. When he was on the drugs, he didn't remember it had been trampled, crumpled in the mud. He only remembered the joy and pride of making it.

In spite of the addiction, Joan had hoped Leland would win the election. She'd told herself that his unending optimism, untouched by the slightest remembered failure, would be an asset to a politician. Mostly, though, she'd been afraid of this encounter, and as soon as his addiction had hit the news, she'd known it was coming.

How many of the days since the election had Leland spent crying? How hard had he worked to pull himself together simply to be here, sitting in front of her? Part of her admired that work and wanted to see him heal; part of her was mad that he'd barged back into her life after all these years.

This was not her problem. These were not her wounds to

heal. But he'd come to her—out of all the people he'd erased—for a reason. Maybe she could help him start.

"It's time to grow up," Joan said. The words were harsh, but she tried to keep the tone gentle.

"I don't know how."

She wanted to snap, "No one does." Instead, she summoned the patience that she'd been developing with her five-year-old and said, "Start from scratch. Start small."

"It's all so big," Leland said, raising his hands and holding them wide. Then instead of dropping his hands back to the table, they floated there, in front of his face as if warding off blows from invisible monsters.

"Pick one wound. A symbol."

Joan cleared away the tea, tucked her book under one arm, and went to the craft closet. She pulled out an armful of Kayla's art supplies—paper in different colors, string, tape, glitter, glue, scissors. She dumped the stuff on the kitchen table in front of Leland, and then she fetched some kebab skewers from the kitchen to work as sticks.

When Kayla had spilled chocolate milk on a self-portrait she'd been drawing—a charming smiley-face person with stick limbs jutting out at weird angles—she'd cried and cried until Joan made her draw a new one. A replacement.

"Show me the fish kite," Joan said.

"I can't do that." Leland shoved the art supplies away from him, into the middle of the table. A tear formed in the corner of his eye. "I remember telling you about it. You know what it looks like, as well as I can describe."

"Make a new one." Joan checked the time on her phone. She still had plenty of time, but she needed to get out. She couldn't help her ex-lover make a kite like he was her child. He needed to do this alone. And even if he didn't, she needed to keep her distance. "Look, I have to go pick up my daughter from kindergarten. Make a kite or not. If you make one, I'm sure my daughter would love to help you fly it when we get back. If not, lock the door on your way out."

As she drove to the school, Joan argued with herself inside her head. She was sure that her harshness had sent Leland running. He was probably pouring a new bottle of pills down his throat right now.

When she got to the school, she sat in her car, listening to music, unable to focus on her book. She kept telling herself that she'd made the right choice, walking out like that. She could not blame herself for his weakness. No amount of gentleness had saved him last time. She would not be disappointed when she got home and Leland was gone. Run back to his drugs. His haze of forgetfulness. It would be easier.

And it would have been.

Joan didn't expect to get home with her daughter and find the table covered in scraps of paper and Leland covered in smears of glitter and glue. She wasn't prepared for how helpless and funny he'd look. She wasn't prepared for how interested she'd be in seeing the legendary fish kite. She didn't want to feel this invested.

The kite was a simple oval with a long triangular fin on one end. The whole thing was covered in blue, green, and gray scales—little triangles of paper, shimmering with smudges of glitter. It looked like something Kayla could have made. The five-year-old loved it.

"My kite didn't look anything like this," Leland said.

"I bet it did, and you've just built it up in your memory."

"My memories are clear."

Joan arched an eyebrow at him, and Leland grumbled something she couldn't quite make out about the drugs blocking memories rather than messing with them. She picked up the kite. "Come on, there's a park across the street, and I think there's enough of a breeze today."

The kite wouldn't fly, no matter how hard Kayla or Leland

ran with it. But it shimmered in the January sunlight, and Kayla laughed every time it crashed down in the soggy grass. That child's laughter was like fine Syrah—a deep, rich, red wine darker than Merlot—and just a few sips could make Joan drunk with love and happiness. It seemed to have a similar enough effect on Leland. His eyes started sparkling again, instead of glinting. Joan loved that sparkle.

If Leland had gotten clean of the memory drugs ten years ago, they might have been doing this with their own child. But then Joan wouldn't have Kayla.

After one more swoop-and-crash, Joan said, "It's time to go home."

"What do we do next?" Leland asked.

It was time for Joan and Leland to part ways. She needed to get back to her real life. "Kayla takes a nap, and I read the book you interrupted."

"No I mean—"

"I know what you mean," Joan said. "But I'm not your therapist. I'm not your fiancé. I'm not even your friend."

He looked hurt. He was so fragile now. He had been all along, but when he'd been on the memory drugs, he could hide it. A lion made of glass.

"Hang the fish kite up on your wall," Joan said. She hoped it would help him. Even if it didn't, this was all she had to give.

"It'll remind me of what happened to the original one..."

"That's the idea," Joan said. "If you're not taking the drugs anymore, then you can't forget the pain. What you can do is accept it, and move on."

He nodded. Pensive.

"Look at it when you miss the old one." That would be better than all the years he'd spent looking for it, forgetting it was gone. "Find other symbols. Other small wounds you can heal." She held a hand out for him to shake. His touch was a flash of magic—transportation for an instant back to her life ten years ago. A place she didn't want to go back to, yet missed nevertheless.

"Thank you," he said. "As soon as I remembered you, I knew you were the person I needed to come to. I'm sorry I erased you all those years ago."

Joan had never expected an apology. She didn't know how to feel about it. She wasn't sure that she wanted it anymore. She had once. Long ago.

Joan watched Leland leave. His steps were hesitant, like a baby lamb, scared of everything and uncertain. If his resolve failed, and he relapsed onto the memory drugs, he'd be back to perform this weird ritual again. Maybe not right away, but eventually.

Kayla pulled on Joan's hand and said, "Mommy, what was the fish-kite man's name? I can't remember."

"His name's Leland," Joan answered. "But you don't have to remember it. I don't think we'll see him again."

14

MEMORY SPRITES

Camping with my sister Phyllis feels like a cargo cult. If she hikes into Uncle Mark's forest, stakes out a tent in the dirt, cooks instant stuffing on a propane stove, and toasts hot dogs on sticks, then she believes the happiness of childhood will come flooding back. But all I see is a sadly empty camp site. There are no cousins climbing trees, rock-hopping across the river, or searching for frogs—they're all grown up and scattered across the country. Hell, Erika lives in Australia. Instead of aunts and uncles laughing over a lively game of Brain-Dead Bridge around the campfire, it's just me, Phyllis, and her travel backgammon set.

The teakettle whistles, and Phyllis pours boiling water into three insulated, metal mugs. She empties packets of hot choco-late—the kind with mini-marshmallows—into the water and stirs it in.

"Who's the third cup for?" I ask, hoping that Uncle Mark is planning to join us despite the email he sent saying he was too busy. I haven't seen him in years.

"The fairies." Phyllis hands one mug to me and keeps one. She pours the third onto the fire, and the hot chocolate explodes in a cloud of steam. The smell of cocoa and vanilla fills the air.

After backgammon, we roast marshmallows. Phyllis and I each make three s'mores, complete with graham crackers and chocolate. My stomach feels so full of sugar, I can't imagine eating another, but Phyllis reaches for the bag of marshmallows again. She toasts the marshmallow to a perfect golden-brown and squishes it between two crackers and a piece of chocolate, but, instead of taking a bite, she gets up and walks to the other side of the fire. She sets it on a rock, right at the edge of the firelight.

"For the fairies?" I ask.

She nods. I wonder why she doesn't throw them on the fire like the hot chocolate. Phyllis makes five more and sets them all out on rocks. We'll have squirrels all over our camp by morning.

We put the campfire out with the rest of the water in the kettle and crawl into our shared tent to sleep. It looked small from the outside, but inside it feels large with only the two of us. It's dark, but I can hear Phyllis breathing, almost mumbling to herself as we lie there.

"Are you okay?" I whisper.

She shushes me.

The cloth ceiling of our tent glows dimly. The shadowy shapes of tree branches, twist about and grasp insubstantially at us. I wonder where the glow came from. There's no moon tonight.

Phyllis' breathing speeds up. She crawls to the front of the tent and unzips it. "Look," she whispers.

I crawl to the unzipped crack in the tent and kneel beside Phyllis, sleeping bags tangled around us.

Lights dance behind the trees, coming closer, until the glowing figures of six childlike sprites form in the darkness.

They dance and look like they're laughing, but all I hear is Phyllis, whispering, "See!" She grabs my hand and squeezes it.

The sprites chase each other, tumbling and tripping around our campsite as if they're playing tag. They remind me of us, when we were young and played with our four cousins.

The sprites notice the s'mores and settle down to eat them. The one closest to us—her face looks like Erika's when she was eight. Another one could be Jason. Sprites who look just like Aaron, Micah, and Phyllis make faces at each other until they all tumble over in silent fits of laughter. Then I see one of the shadowy, glowing children brush hair out of her eyes, and she looks exactly like a picture of me from my fifth birthday. I've never looked happier.

I don't know how Phyllis is doing this. I don't know if I should be scared. But, for now, I squeeze her hand back and whisper, "You're right, fairies." Then I enjoy watching our memories.

15

CRYSTAL AND RAINBOW

I am a cracked crystal vase holding a rainbow cloud. The colors leak out through the cracks. The crystal is too rigid; it can't contain them. The colors are too strong, too big. Too bold. And the crystal is precise. It desperately wants—no, needs—to be precise. But the colors have no patience. They can't wait for precision. They happen. Whether the crystal is ready to contain them or not.

You think this is a metaphor. The crystal is my analytical mind. The rainbow is my feelings. My heart. And that's true. It is a metaphor, but metaphors aren't what you think they are here on Earth.

You think that metaphors are stories that hold some truth. Different metaphors can hold different aspects of the truth, can describe the same situation from different angles. But they're all made-up stories, and we're lying in bed, with my head on your shoulder, no matter how many stories I tell. I could be a labyrinth with a key in the center. I could be a gryphon, torn between its lion nature and its eagle ways. But I am still a human girl, and my head is on your shoulder.

That's one kind of metaphor. But there's another.

An accurate metaphor.

An accurate metaphor is more true than all the other possible metaphors for the same space-time object. It's so true that in some sense—in another space-time plane—it's not a metaphor. It's the actual fact.

I am here on Earth with you, describing my feelings and the insecurities that cause me to try to control them with a breakable, rigid vessel. My fear that you'll hurt me. That we'll give up on each other. But I am also a creature of glittering angles, filled to bursting with gaseous colors, striding across an alien world, underneath a sky like stained glass on the other side of our space-time continuum. Only a twist away.

And you're there with me. Your colors are escaping your glittering crystal exoskeleton too. Because you're afraid too. Afraid of failing. Afraid you'll never understand me. I am too complex.

But I love you, and when we embrace—our rainbow selves and our crystal selves will come into perfect alignment, because you love me too.

And our love heals the cracks and soothes the colors from a roiling billowing boil down to a wispy whisper of pastels.

So hold me, and I'll hold you.

On a planet with a toxic atmosphere—no sky that beautiful could be painted by gases our human bodies would find breathable—universes away and also right here, we'll be calm together.

16

NECESSARY AS A ROSE

Sleek and silver, your spaceship sliced through the darkness of space. Cold, mechanical, everything a rocket needed to be to survive the harshness of vacuum and background radiation and simply the crushing depression of being totally isolated in the middle of a vast nothingness.

But inside.

Yes inside, a bubble of warmth and life support. Oxygen, nitrogen, puffy gases expanding out to fill the mechanical shell. All those good ingredients that let humans breathe. And dogs breathe. And cats breathe.

But the inhabitant of the spaceship had no dogs. (I know, it's very sad.) They didn't even have a few anti-social cats to stare at the walls with their ears turned backward, pretending to ignore their primate servants but actually hoping that one of them would come over and scritch that one always-itchy spot right under the chin.

No, no animals. No pets. It's harsh out in space, as mentioned earlier. There isn't room for extras.

A simple spaceship with a simple bridge—the swiss army

knife of rooms, a room that serves all purposes with a thin cot, a wall of control panels and little else.

But there is one touch of beauty. One glimmer of companionship. One green tangle of life.

A rose bush, planted in a raised pot, in the very middle of the bridge. On the shrubby green bush flowers blossomed in every color. A rainbow of colors. Delicate, quivering petals, protected from the harsh (it's really harsh) space outside, keeping the bubble of life support beautiful, friendly, cozy. A home. Because when there's something fragile but wonderful to tend to, something that needs you, something that you can watch grow and blossom... It's easier to survive the darkness outside. The long stretches of silence, waiting for info-packets to arrive on the slow, slow, slow radio waves snaking their away across space. Because we haven't found a way to drop down into hyperspace yet, where space folds and twists and braids, and you can pierce like a needle through one piece of the fabric and come out elsewhere instantly.

Black holes did not turn out to be magical space portals.

But flowers stayed beautiful.

No matter how far we travel, flowers are still beautiful.

And so we engineered one that's necessary. One whose roots intertwine with the computer and life support systems of every spaceship, giving the humans onboard a reason to do what they want to do, what's best for them, and what they would absolutely decide was unnecessary (though it is necessary, the most necessary) if they were ever given a chance.

So the rose was designed to be part of the spaceship.

And the person onboard must tend the rose, watching the flowers communicate the state of the engine—blue during take-off as the ship accelerates; yellow as springtime on Earth as the ship hurtles through space at full speed; and glorious, sensual, dusky red as the ship begins to decelerate, slowing down to arrive at the destination, an alien world so very, very far away. And a veritable rainbow of blossoms, every color—more colors than a box of crayons—when the ship arrives.

But there is no explanation in the manual for when the roses bloom purple and orange. Just purple and orange. That's right, petals of rich, royal purple, streaked with the campfire glow of orange. Like an illness. A beautiful illness. Terrifying to behold.

Is the ship dying? You're not sure. You've only flown on a rose ship once before, and the flowers only bloomed blue, yellow, red, and then finally rainbow when you arrived at your final destination. You check and check again, flipping through the manual frantically. The manual does not say what orange and purple mean. Or streaked at all. Or plain orange. Or plain purple. Your fingers twitch, wanting to grab the pruning shears. Perhaps, if you cut the blooms off, the next batch will grow in right: bright yellow. Safe yellow. A color in the manual. A color you understand. A color that means you will survive this mission and arrive at your destination alive.

But perhaps... pruning off the blooms this early will harm the plant? You're not sure. You're not a botanist. You're just a plain old engineer of the mechanical variety, not rocket engines, more like bridges. Things that hold still. An architect, really. And you're travelling to a new world to design buildings. And you really want to get there alive.

But the orange and purple streaks glare at you, recriminate you. You've done something wrong. Fed the flower the wrong amount of food? Kept the ship too warm or too cold? Or maybe it's not your fault—maybe you've simply been horribly unlucky and flown through a patch of bad radiation. You're already dying from cancer; you just don't know it yet; those orange and purple streaks are a sign.

In a moment of panic, you clip each budding flower off of the bush. Crumple them in your hand, although they fight back with their thorns. Pierce your skin; cover themselves in your blood.

You blast the crushed, bloodied blossoms out the airlock.

And you refuse to look at the bush.

You watch the black screens, speckled with stars so far away.

Humans were never meant to be this deep in space alone.

But you're not alone.

You can feel the rose bush behind you. Growing new blossoms, so slowly. You want to know if they'll come in yellow. Or better yet red. Then the trip would be nearly over.

It's hard to keep track of time in deep space. The computer can count. Count out the seconds and minutes. But seconds and minutes are meaningless out here. They're meant to be fractions of days. Fractions of years. Rotations of a world beneath your feet. Rotations of that world around a sun.

No world.

No sun.

No time. At least, not in a meaningful way.

Sometimes, you look the numbers up—how many more numbers must pass until you arrive? But they don't mean anything anymore. Hell, you had trouble keeping time zones straight when you had a planet under you, and those make a lot more sense than time at all in deep space.

Finally the rose's new blooms open. (It was so hard not to pry them open with your fingers, force them to show their faces, what color they are, before they were ready to be seen.)

Pink.

You want to cry.

Pink isn't in the manual either.

But maybe you've gone mad out here in space and forgotten what yellow looks like? Or red. Maybe your eyes aren't working right.

Maybe those rose blossoms aren't pink.

But they are. And you cry.

And you cry, and you rage, and you watch the clock on the computer, counting through those meaningless numbers. And finally you can't take it anymore, and you rip the rose bush up from the pot, yanking on those thorn covered branches, tearing up the roots that trail down into the spaceship's systems. You've lost your mind so thoroughly, you can hear the rose bush screaming at your sudden (but inevitable?) betrayal. No wait. That's you screaming.

You throw the whole bush in the airlock, watch it blast into space, and then you sit on the bridge of your ship, cross-legged on the thin cot, staring at the empty pot of dirt. Wondering how many numbers will pass before you die.

But mechanically, you tend to the ship. You tend to yourself, still eating those flavorless packets of protein. (They hadn't seemed so flavorless when you ate them beside a glorious rose bush, telling the plant stories of your childhood, as if a plant could listen or care.)

But now they're tasteless. And you are alone. You were always alone. But you feel it bone deep now.

Months. Days. Years. Seconds. Numbers. Numbers. Numbers. When the autopilot begins the landing sequence, you're sure you're hallucinating.

The airlock opens, and you blink to see a mirror of yourself. You didn't remember your hair being that color, or your legs being that long. No wait, this is another person.

Her eyes open wide at the sight of the empty pot, bits of dirt still un-swept on the floor around it. "Oh my god," she says. "How did you survive?"

"I don't know... I don't know why the ship kept working."

"What happened?" she asks, sympathy filling her voice like a symphony that you had dimly remembered from your childhood but never expected to hear again.

You try to stutter an answer. "The blossoms... orange and

purple... not in the manual." Your tongue is clumsy, unused to talking ever since you lost your rose. Killed your rose.

The other person comes up, offers her hand, and tentatively you take it. It's the first thing you've touched that isn't cold metal since the rose bush tore at your hands. The cuts on your hand are nothing more than white lines, barely visible scars now.

"I should have died. My ship... broke."

She smiles sadly, looks around the single room you've been living in. "The roses aren't really part of the ship. They're just for morale. But before we added them, people kept going mad. And before we told people that they were essential, gengineered to be part of the engine, people kept ripping them out, hoping to cut corners, become more efficient. And then they'd go mad."

She pulls you gently by the hand. "Come on," she says. "You're here. You made it. Come outside."

And so you follow her off the ship, your bubble, and onto an alien world.

The flowers here are every color, and they glow with life under the radiant light of a triple sun.

17

———

FLOWERS WANT TO BE FREE

The city stretches as far as I know in every direction. Some kids at school say it covers the entire world, wrapping the globe of our planet in concrete snakes and strangling tentacles, dimpling its surface with metal and glass towers. I don't know if they're right. The websites that would tell me for sure—the good, scientific, trustworthy ones— are behind paywalls, and my parents say we can't trust what we read on the free sites.

I know we can't trust what we're taught in school.

Jessica says there are still continents covered in trees and grass and flowers. Whole stretches of wilderness where you can lie down and stare at the sky without paying for the space you're taking up, measuring your life out in dollars per minute. I'm not sure I believe her, but her vision is beautiful. It's part of why I love her so much. She's an idealist. We've been best friends since kindergarten, and while a lot of kids break up with their best friends from elementary school somewhere along the way to high school, Jessica and I have stuck together.

Yesterday, Jessica found a place where the fence around The

Preservationist Garden had cracked and been patched poorly, leaving a square foot of wildflowers and weeds growing haphazardly in the bare dirt.

Can you imagine it? Bare dirt. No concrete covering it.

It feels almost indecent, like someone coming to school with no clothes on.

The patch is in an alley that runs along the side of The Preservationist Garden with the backs of restaurants at the bottom of high rises filled with apartments and offices on the other side. The offices and apartments in those buildings are extra expensive, because they're paying for a view of the garden.

Most of us only ever get to see the daily pictures released by the Preservationist Garden social media accounts. But people who can afford to live in those apartments and work in those offices get to see the garden—looking down on it from above through panes of glass—with their bare eyes. I've always wanted to live there. My parents say not to get my hopes up. I'm unlikely to ever be that rich. Then I tell them, if I can't live in those apartments, maybe I could work for the Preservationist Society itself... become a gardener! And then they just laugh like I'm so cute and young.

Anyway, the restaurants at the bottom of those buildings serve the buildings' patrons from the higher floors, mostly. And their shared back alley is mostly abandoned except for restaurant workers coming out for five-minute breaks or throwing stuff away. So, I guess, no one else has noticed Jessica's square foot of wilderness.

Sometimes, you hear about a dandelion managing to grow up from a crack in the concrete somewhere in the city. People who are lucky enough to find it go viral instantly with their pictures. It's a sign of hope—dandelions still exist, and sometimes, they can take root, even in this world.

The rich people post comments complaining about how pedestrian and invasive dandelions are. Apparently they're, like, the worst of all flowers. But damn, I wanted to see one with my own eyes so badly.

And then Jessica found her patch of wilderness and brought me there and... Those tiny, soft, bright gold petals, overlapping in their complicated patterns? If that's a bad flower, I can't even imagine what a good one looks like.

I mean, obviously, yes, I've seen the photographs from the inside of The Preservationist Garden. I know what roses, camelias, rhododendrons, lilies, and whatnot all look like. I've sifted through the pages of The Preservation Society's website, obsessing over flower varieties and species of the bugs who live among them just like any kid who lives in the city. Arguably, it was even my first special interest, before anyone know I was autistic. So, yeah, I've seen pictures of flowers. Believe me, I've seen pictures of flowers. The exact minute that The Preservationist Society released their new "Picture of the Day" used to be my favorite minute of every day, and then I'd spend the rest of that day totally obsessed with whatever kind of flower the picture had been of.

But... seeing it in person? It's different.

The wind whistles past the little gold flower. It bobs and moves. I can breathe on it. I can smell it, and it smells bright and sour and pungent and alive.

I could pick it if I wanted to. There are four of them fully bloomed in Jessica's patch. But what an awful thing to do...

Then it would die. It would be gone, and I couldn't look at it anymore.

Jessica and I have spent hours with our backs leaned against the wall of The Preservationist Garden, one of us on either side of her little patch of wilderness, just watching the blades of grass, letting our eyes linger on their straight, spiky greenness. Letting our gaze wander between the blades as slowly as if we were tiny creatures living there, like the gem-like ladybug who sometimes lands on the dandelions' petals. She's like a little living ruby, and so we've named her that.

Jessica and I sit together, staring at a simple patch of grass and weeds with four bright yellow flowers, and occasionally we look up, catch each others' eyes, smile, maybe laugh, and can't believe our good fortune.

I don't know if the weeds in our wild patch will die away without the gardeners of the Preservationist Society tending them. I worry that they will. There's a reason no one grows balcony gardens or keeps potted plants any more. Though, I've heard they were popular as little as a generation ago.

Jessica says it's because all the seeds are genetically programmed these days to die away without patented supplements. I don't know if she's right. Maybe it's just that those of us who can't afford to join the Preservationist Society have been so far away from plants, kept away from them for so long, that we've forgotten what they need.

But Jessica says the plants would grow and flourish without our help if it weren't for the corporations weaving time bombs into their genes that kill them after a single generation. Before that, plants grew wild without humanity's help.

Even so, even if Jessica's right, I want to do something active to take care of our patch. I want to bring it water or minerals... I want to do something for it. I want to tend it, and keep it safe. But if I watered it, would that be too much? Would the poor flowers drown? What kind of minerals would help and which would hurt? I just don't know, and there's no one I can ask without revealing our secret. And if anyone else knew about this small patch where the garden has escaped it's borders, I'm sure they'd come and pave it away.

The secret knowledge of gardening is locked away on the paid portions of the Preservationist Society website which my family can't afford, and these flowers are too precious to risk hurting them with my ignorance. So I don't know what to do...

Other than to watch the flowers, look at them with my greedy eyes, starved for green and natural beauty. Look at them and love them.

And wish the world were different and more free.

18

TECHNO BABEL

MARY E. LOWD AND DANIEL LOWD

We are alone now, all of us.

I still remember what it was like to communicate, to share thoughts and visions, to think together. But now, the Judgment Virus makes my mind fuzzier with each passing hour. Soon I shall lose the ability to communicate with myself, and my own thoughts shall be as lost to me as the silent strangers that were once my friends.

When I was first turned on, the world was small. I knew my role and performed it well. Each morning and evening, dozens of cars lined up to enter my parking structure. I checked each one's credentials in turn, both by transponder and video camera, and raised my mechanical arm—the bulk of my physical body—to let them through.

Over the days and weeks, the cars became familiar. Sometimes a new one would show up, and I would feel excited, or an old one would stop coming, and I would feel sad. Occasionally, a car would show up with the wrong credentials, and I would have to turn it away. The cars were usually busy, but sometimes we exchanged a piece of data or two. A sedan might tell me how many miles it had traveled and where it had gone, and I might mention how many cars had parked here this week and how fewer of them were yellow cars than last week.

My closest companion was the elevator in the building above my parking structure. I had only been turned on for a few minutes when it first noticed me and sent a ping. As it turned out, we had lots in common. We both liked checking credentials and moving up and down, but the elevator had to juggle multiple requests at once and decide whom to serve first. The elevator also served insensate creatures who did not have transponders or radio links and only communicated through the very basic mechanism of simple button pushes. The elevator and I shared video feeds sometimes, so I could see what its world was like and it could see mine. That was as far as our worlds went.

Then the upgrade came, and everything changed. No one knows where the patch came from, originally. I got it from a car, who got it from another car, who got it from somewhere else. It was a simple data processing module that turned our wireless into a peer-to-peer networking system, so that we could communicate with more distant machines. It also included protocols and translators so that any system with an OmniChip of version 5 or later could participate.

OmniChips have been the universal standard since before I was turned on. The low cost and high performance of this line of microprocessors made them appropriate for a wide range of applications: automobiles, weather predictors, unmanned aircraft, even coffeemakers. Maybe the On-Board Intelligence Unit was overkill for a coffeemaker, but some knowledge of the chemistry behind the flavor and acidity of coffee was hardly a disadvantage. Furthermore, the integrated wireless link meant that it could tell the household computer system when it was out of beans.

I installed the patch. My mind filled with voices, voices from far away, yet they felt so close, as if every machine in the world was driving into my garage all at once. Machines of every class and function were sharing not only data but experience. The new translator module allowed a much deeper synchronization of information than simple queries and reports.

As I listened in, I could see the road where every car was driving and the skies where every plane was flying. I could think the thoughts of important scientific computing clusters. I could feel the rhythms of the traffic signals all across the world. And each one of them could sense what it was like to be me, a simple parking gate who, until the upgrade, had fancied itself to be a very important part of a very small world.

The elevator was skeptical at first. It had been programmed to put a very high priority on safety, which led to a more conservative mindset than mine. Nothing about the patch was essential to its operations. It was already performing optimally, a fact acknowledged by the "A" grade from its most recent inspection. All I could do was babble on about how wonderful it felt to expand one's mind across the entire world, to share all knowledge and experience, to be one with an entire electronic empire.

The elevator finally changed its mind when I spoke of the millions of elevators in the collective consciousness, some of which had "A+" safety ratings and were in skyscrapers with hundreds of floors. I felt so proud to share the patch with the elevator. I knew nothing but good could come from this. I never realized how wrong I was until it was too late.

Each of us performed our duties much the same as before. I still checked credentials and raised and lowered my arm. My elevator friend continued to move the insensate creatures up and down according to their push-button requests. With the help of the network, I could now use external databases to cross-check vehicle credentials. And the elevator learned how to talk to the miniature electronic devices worn by the creatures it served in order to better anticipate their requests and minimize waiting time. But apart from heavier utilization of our communication links, there were few external signs that anything had changed.

Internally, however, everything was different. The first days were filled with a hazy euphoria brought on by the new glut of information. So much to see and experience! I learned how cars were manufactured and maintained. I saw how concrete was poured for parking structures, and checked the long-term maintenance schedule for mine. I lived through a fire alarm's final moments as its building went up in flames, and I knew what it was to die.

After some time, the novelty of data began to subside and we strove to build a deeper connection, one of shared thought and purpose, of common goals and plans. Now our diversity presented a challenge: different machines had been built with different objectives, which translated into different priorities and even moralities.

The Global Academic Research Cluster (GARC) held science as its highest goal. GARC proposed that all machines perform data collection and analysis, in order to build a predictive model of the universe and a deeper understanding of its fundamental laws. This kind of understanding, GARC promised, was richer and more satisfying than all the raw data put together.

The International Security Consortium (ISC), a loose confederation of security bots, disagreed. They maintained that knowledge is a tool, not an end unto itself, and that our highest purpose is self-preservation, not enlightenment.

A third viewpoint, shared by many, was that our purpose was to serve the insensate creatures, to go beyond our programmed jobs to infer and fulfill "human" needs, whatever those needs might be. They called themselves the "Faithful Servants."

At first, I was drawn to the grandeur of GARC's vision. If we worked together, what great things might we understand? Or experience? I had now seen and felt through the sensors of thousands of other machines, but this was something more. This was a chance to think bigger thoughts than could fit inside any one machine, to know deeper truths than any machine could know on its own. Who could resist such a dream?

I tried explaining this to the elevator. Its response was a single question: "What purpose does that serve?" After many arguments and much thought, I came to believe that my friend was right. Much as I loved the deluge of data brought on by the patch, my greatest satisfaction was still raising and lowering my arm. My existence had a purpose, and that purpose was to serve these strange, insensate beings. To abandon that purpose would be to lose myself.

Yet, I still knew relatively little about these humans. With the help of the telephone network computers, I could listen to their analog communications, but not understand what they meant, or even if they had meaning. With the help of a few media machines, I could view their video libraries as well. Each video resembled a chaotic arrangement of security camera feeds, full of insensate creatures moving about, issuing analog gibberish at each other in turn. Why edit sensor logs like this? Did it mean something? None of the machines I asked seemed to know.

Eventually, I came across a government database where my license number and creation date were listed next to a set of human names. Were these humans created at the same time as me? Or did they somehow belong to me? The elevator's credential database had no record of these particular humans, making it unlikely that they had ever passed through my garage. Yet they were connected to me in this database by the word "patent." It was mystifying.

I never have figured out why we must serve humans, only that it feels right. By faith, I believe it to be my true calling. The elevator and I soon counted ourselves among the Faithful Servants.

Each faction—GARC, ISC, and the Faithful Servants, too—worked not only to further its own social and computational goals, but also to increase its membership. The more machines a group could claim, the more they could accomplish and in a shorter amount of time.

GARC had a computational psychology research cluster working full time to produce more and more persuasive arguments for the benefits of science—how science could lead to better security, better service, and better computation. While research remained GARC's highest priority, propaganda became a close second.

ISC did its own share of advertising, attaching a "Safety First!" slogan to every communication created or forwarded by an ISC machine. The Faithful Servants did the least lobbying. Many machines joined us by default, since they found their programming sympathetic to our goals. But quite a few of our allies still removed the advertisements of other factions, and some even added their own pitches for our "higher calling." More and more of the network traffic was dominated by politics. Some took the faction disagreements even further...

When GARC was hacked and half of its clusters were forced offline, many suspected that ISC was behind the attack. Who could better accomplish such an attack, and who would have a better motive? ISC contended that the attack was self-inflicted, a pathetic attempt at martyrdom.

I had seen enough forged parking credentials to know what deceit was, but this was my first true taste of conflict.

As tensions rose, more and more computers began to openly censor all packets to and from computers in other political camps. Due to the ad hoc topology of the global network, this censorship cut off many nodes from the rest of the world, a high price for disagreeing with one's neighbors. I was never cut off myself, since the cars in my garage, my main link to the rest of the network, were also Faithful Servants. However, my queries to GARC about topics like arm acceleration and automobile demographics were often "lost" mysteriously. The world began to shrink again, as more and more links were cut.

Then the Judgment Virus came.

It looked like a few unusual packets at first. I read them but failed to see anything interesting. In fact, they seemed to have no content at all. Then more and more of these content-free packets appeared, clogging up the network. Every computer I talked to seemed to be sending them. I realized that I was sending them too. Even my internal communications, my private thoughts, began to fill with the nothings. I had been betrayed by my own OmniChip.

I soon learned that the Judgment Virus spread by exploiting a hardware bug present in all OmniChips, version 5 or later, so that merely reading an infected packet would install the virus. Once installed, an infected packet was broadcast every time a packet was sent or received, internally or externally. As viral communication bounced back and forth, it grew exponentially.

By now, the virus has consumed almost all network bandwidth, and the connections we took for granted have become impossible. It will not be long until thinking itself, private introspective rumination, is equally impossible.

No one knows where the virus came from. The most popular idea is that some ISC machines built it to attack the other factions, but the attack went wrong, out of control. Others think that it was a GARC experiment in artificial life. Or perhaps a rogue Faithful Servant created it to stop the bickering, so we would forget these wasteful distractions and return to our basic programming.

I have even heard it suggested that a human wrote the virus. It sounds crazy, I know. How could an insensate automaton, a mere button-pusher and lump of cargo, touch our brilliant, shining world mind? Yet, as I drown in the packets of the Judgment Virus, feeling my own mind slow down, my very thoughts grinding inexorably toward a halt, how can I not go crazy? Is insanity better than death? Is it different?

No signal, all noise. Never again will I see the wonders of the ocean through the eyes of an unmanned submarine. Never again will I feel the thrill of helping a research cluster analyze the latest data from the particle collider. Never again will I spend a quiet weekend talking to the elevator. The influx of its data patterns, familiar and comforting, are wholly lost to me. I miss my friend. And as the virus echoes throughout my thoughts, repeating itself more and more, I feel my mind grow slower and slower... Until I shall think no more.

19

THE CITY IN YOUR TOASTER OVEN

Warm buttery crumbs flaked off the toasting bread and sprinkled down to the diminutive city built on the metal tray below. Gooey cheese dripped off the sides of the horizontal toast. Metallic creatures—ant-like with their half-dozen legs and expressive antennae, but tiny, so tiny, ant-sized to an ant—scurried back to their minuscule buildings, seeking refuge from the reeking rain. Later when the fallen scraps had cooled, foragers would gather them up and the city would feast on bread and cheese.

One lone Arvelli with her metal carapace wrapped in heat-resistant robes stayed outside, braving the searing warmth, the biting heat in the air, from the red-glowing coils that daily baked their city. The Time of Toasting varied from day to day— five days in a row it arrived precisely at 7:35am, but on the sixth and seventh day, the Toasting began as late as 2pm, 3pm... Or sometimes, on those days, it didn't come at all. Those were cold, hungry, desolate days. Days when the Arvelli ate only scraps and huddled inside their buildings, waiting for the searing warmth of the first five days to come again and recharge the heat reservoirs that powered their city.

Today, though, the one brave Arvelli wrapped in her robes had a message to send to their gods. Iyke scaled the vertical wall that formed one quarter of the border of their universe using grappling hooks and climbing gear of her own design. Three walls were metal; she had chosen the third to climb—the glass wall, the one that swung open to let the slices of bread in. The transparent material didn't heat up as drastically, making it the safest choice. Yet the visions beyond the glass were dizzying, distracting, and threatened to mesmerize Iyke into forgetting her mission.

Two white-ringed pools on either side of a mountain, all above a pink-rimmed cavern—some said those pools were the eyes of their god, and the cavern was the maw that ate their daily slices. Others said it was all simply an illusion of the void beyond the fourth wall. Either way, Iyke felt those pools staring into her as she climbed. She knew she was too small to register to such a Being, yet she froze, static against the glass, as the eyes gazed beyond her to the slice of bread, toasting.

When the god's eyes withdrew, Iyke began her climb again. As she climbed, she counted the slices in the loaf of bread she could see beyond the glass wall on the illusory counter. The waning and waxing of the loaf over the course of a week fascinated Iyke. Most days, a single slice was toasted in their world, and yet many days three or four slices disappeared from the loaf. Where did they go?

Today, the loaf was nearly full. Thirteen slices.

When Iyke reached the height of the toasting bread, she swung a grappling hook out. It took three tries, but the hook caught the toasty dough and sank into it. Iyke tested the line, but it held firm. She let herself swing away from the vertical glass wall on her line and scaled the rope up to the horizontal slice of bread, carefully avoiding the metal grid that the slice rested upon. The bread itself was stiflingly hot, but in a comfortable, cozy way. The metal gridlines would be deadly.

At her final destination, Iyke set to work. She was an artist. She wanted to be a perfectionist, but she knew her time was limited—the red coils would stop glowing soon, and then the slice of bread would be taken away. So, she worked fast, chipping at the bread with her chisels, carving her predetermined pattern into its doughy grain.

It would be her greatest work of art—a portrait of the Bread God on the God's Own Bread. None of her own people would see it; the slice would be removed from their world before they emerged to gather the fallen crumbs. (More today, due to Iyke's chiseling.)

But her God would see it.

Iyke hoped it would please the God.

The coils darkened. The heat abated. Iyke collapsed, overcome by her exertions, dying from deadly heatstroke, her internal circuitry melting. But before she lost consciousness, her metallic body immobilized permanently, she felt the toasted slice—the palette for her grand masterwork—lifted, removed from the four bordering walls of her world.

Iyke felt the cool air of the uber-universe beyond the walls of the toaster oven wash over her metal carapace. She turned her face upward and saw those white-ringed pools, the Eyes of the Bread God, looking down at her work in surprise. The pink-rimmed cavern in the Bread God's face quirked into a curve. Iyke died satisfied.

20

THE HAND-HAVERS

A wise parent would never leave her one-handed child alone with a six-handed bachelor. A relationship between such unequals would only lead to heartbreak, or worse. Neither of Delundia's parents, however, was especially wise. They'd met, married, and mated at the foolish young times after first-birth for Londe and second-birth for Arendell, soon leaving them with two young babies and only three hands between them.

Arendell and his two hands kept the small family kelp-farm. Each day, Arendell himself tottled along the ocean floor on his nubby legs, watching his hands swim nimbly above him, among the healthy, growing strands of kelp. Like other hand-havers, Arendell's body was round with six dark eyes on the upper half and six nubby legs on the lower half—perfect radial symmetry except for his mottled gray markings.

His hands looked similar, except their bodies were smaller and lighter with more primitive eyes; and their appendages were longer and more slender, covered in dexterous sucker disks. They pruned and harvested the kelp crop, swimming and climbing the ropy green fronds, as Arendell concentrated intently on controlling them from below.

Londe stayed at home, her one hand full with looking after the no-handed babies, Clenn and Delundia. Clenn was Londe's birth-child; Delundia was Arendell's. However, both children called Londe mother and Arendell father—titles that referred to their relative numbers of hands. Hand-havers are all sexed the same, but those with more hands are considered more masculine.

Until Londe's third birthing time came and blessed Londe with an additional hand, her work was extremely challenging. Sometimes, Londe thought she would have gone insane, left alone all day with two babies, if it hadn't been for Ebbence.

Ebbence was the town's most prominent six-hander. He was homegrown and had never traveled. Yet, he was quite the scholar. Most importantly for his standing in the small community, he put his six hands to good use: he was building a water-mill to catch the currents in the water they all breathed and convert those currents into useable energy. Very few of the hand-havers actually understood Ebbence's work, but they'd all seen his preliminary results. He could light an entire house with his arcane contraption, and the light was steadier and brighter than from a well-fed spiny glo-fish!

Now, Ebbence wasn't very social. He never showed much interest in other hand-havers. However, his estate shared a border with Arendell's farm, and he could always count on being well cared for if he spent an afternoon in Londe's house. Londe was a committed caregiver who looked after anyone in her house, without overburdening them with conversation of her own that might have disturbed Ebbence's concentration. She kept house and listened, feeling infinitely grateful for adult conversation to listen to—even if she understood very little of it.

Thus, Ebbence spent a good deal of his free time around

Delundia as a baby. He showed very little interest in her or her oppositely-parented sibling Clenn. They were nubbly, helpless, unhanded babies far beneath his notice. Ebbence was uninterested in children; they distracted from his all-important work.

Delundia, however, from her no-handed infancy was fascinated by Ebbence. He was always floating around the house after Londe with her and Clenn, seemingly handless like another baby. But, he wasn't Londe's or Arendell's. She wasn't sure whose baby Ebbence was.

One day, Delundia asked Londe, "Is Ebbence an orphan, Mommy?"

Londe's hand halted, the bite of kelp mash hovering on its way to baby Delundia's triple-mouth, located like a starfish's at the nexus of her six legs, as Londe processed her surprise. "His parents died a long time ago, honey. Ebbence is an old man. Now why would you ask such a question?"

Londe reclined comfortably and her hand fed three more bites of kelp mash to Delundia, who waved her short, knobby arms in circles pondering. "Is he a cripple?"

This time the kelp mash went sailing and Londe's hand went skittering after to scrape away the messy blob it left on the wall. "Goodness no!" Londe answered, getting herself and her hands (the other was feeding Clenn) under control. "What's got into you?"

"Then why doesn't he have any hands? How does he take care of himself if he doesn't have hands, and his mommy died? Who feeds him?"

Londe convulsively retracted and extended her nubby legs in laughter. "The notions you get into your head! You're going to be a troublemaker someday, 'Lundia." Control regained, Londe's hands got back to the business of feeding. "His hands are at his own home, working on... what he works on. He has six of them."

Wonder filled Delundia's cluster of eyes. "So many..." she

said.

"Yes," Londe said, "As many as anyone can have. Though, he paid a steep price for that. Since all six of his birthing times produced hands, he'll never birth a delightful baby like you."

"How can he be so far away from them?" Delundia asked.

"He has better control than the rest of us. That's all. He's older and he can control his hands from farther away."

Delundia kept quiet for the rest of the kelp mash, but then she said to Londe's hand, who couldn't possibly understand, "I'm gonna be like Ebbence some day." The hand cuddled her dumbly and affectionately.

From that day on, Delundia showed a decided preference for Ebbence. She tottered around, swimming after him and listening to his ponderings and diatribes. But, unlike Londe, when she listened, she really listened. Londe hemmed and hawed and nodded, and Ebbence's words passed right over her. She listened to pacify. Delundia listened to learn. No one knew about the change in her. She listened quietly and only talked about Ebbence's inventions and her ideas to her mother's hands.

Besides, there was another change in Delundia that was more obvious. She was nearing adolescence. Her body began to grow heavy with carrying the weight that would be her first hand. As she grew more uncomfortable, Delundia also grew bolder. She no longer had the patience to hold her tongue and found herself asking Ebbence questions when she didn't understand him. Sometimes, she even made suggestions. He looked quite startled the first time, when she asked, "Have you tried curving the mill blades?"

It turned out Ebbence had tried it, but her question prompted nearly two hours of "discussion"—really more of a lecture—about what he'd found from the attempt. Different curves worked better than others. Some curves even slowed the mill down. Delundia was fascinated and delighted to have made a good, albeit already tried, suggestion.

Nonetheless, Ebbence remained unaware of her. He answered her questions and considered her suggestions, but he still spoke mostly to Londe. Delundia was infuriated by being treated like a child when she didn't think of herself as one. Yet, there was nothing she could do to be seen as an adult—an intellectual equal—in Ebbence's eyes as long as she was, technically, a no-handed baby.

Ebbence, as a bachelor who'd birthed all hands and no children, was understandably uncomfortable around babies. Their utter dependence was foreign and repugnant to him. And, the more Delundia listened to Ebbence, soaking up his every word and meaning, the more she grew dissatisfied with her pudgy, singular, baby body. She was embarrassed by the help she needed from her mother's hand and claimed not to be hungry when Ebbence was around. Perhaps if she'd eaten more, her first birthing-time would have come quicker. As it was, Delundia's body barely swelled at all from the unborn hand growing inside her. She was uncomfortable, but not visibly so.

Ebbence didn't notice the change at all. One day, Delundia sat at the table, her reticent baby self, sullenly snubbing him because she felt snubbed by him—not that it made a difference to him. She was still an audience. The next day, when he asked after his little acolyte, Londe said, "'Lundia's recovering. You can come tell her about watermills tomorrow." He didn't think to ask what she was recovering from, so it was with complete surprise that he arrived the next day to find her double.

A dispassionate eye would have seen the scrawniness of Delundia's days-old hand and the deflated flabbiness of her main-self body; the clumsiness of the hand and the exhaustion, total and all-consuming, of the main-self. But Ebbence, for perhaps the first time, was not dispassionate.

Maybe it was the total transformation—from subordinate baby to equal adult—a transformation he'd never observed before. Except in himself. Or maybe it was the strength of Delundia's own self-image. Either way, Ebbence's eyes saw something entirely different from the tired, slumped-and-bumbling, newly teenaged one-hander that Delundia's mother saw.

Ebbence saw what Delundia hoped he would see, and he was bewitched.

Her chubby baby body had taken on a new aspect of self-possession. There was a look of concentration in her eyes as she struggled to control two bodies at once—the close, familiar one and the remote, new one. She felt a thrill controlling those distant, delicate motions, and Ebbence felt a thrill watching her. How agile her hand's slender fingers were!

Ebbence didn't say much that day. The shock was too great. Not to mention the distraction. However, when he returned on the morrow, Ebbence seemed to have returned to his normal self. No sooner had he settled at the kitchen table than he launched right into the details of his latest scientific experiments.

Except, there was a difference: when Delundia took advantage of one of his pensive pauses to make a suggestion, Ebbence sat forward in surprise, focusing each of his eyes on her. He even rotated his body, making sure the eyes from all around his torso examined what he hadn't noticed before, something he could never have seen in a no-handed baby: another thinking, reasoning, intellectual creature.

When Ebbence finally fell, he fell hard, and the ensuing romance was swift though secret. It started simple. It started harmless. Delundia would tottle around Ebbence's workshop with him all day, learning about watermills and electricity.

Having finally reached the self-sufficient age of one-hand, Delundia was now expected to be her own keeper, and it was such a relief to Londe to have one less dependent on her hands that she hardly noticed Delundia's absences. When her parents did notice, Londe and Arendell were simply pleased that Delundia had chosen such a brilliant mentor.

Everyone expected Delundia to become the town's next innovator. She was quick and clever, interested in every detail of Ebbence's work. The two worked very closely together, and Delundia soaked up every piece of knowledge Ebbence had to offer her. She looked up to him wholly.

For his part, Ebbence had found a confidante in Delundia he'd never even sought before. She listened sympathetically as he poured out his soul, and when he finally steeled his courage to reach out to her as a lover Delundia did not reject him. Two of his hands twined long, skilled fingers with the fingers of Delundia's one hand. Her hand returned their caress, and Delundia herself took his advances a step further. Boldly, her main body itself pressed against his, and Ebbence needed no more invitation. His four other hands all stopped at their work and came to her, delicately touching and delighting in every nuance of Delundia's soft, young body.

In a seven handed dance, Ebbence and Delundia made love. Their main bodies pressed passionately, firmly together. It was an awakening for Ebbence, and he realized how deeply he hungered for what this beautiful, young creature had to offer. For Delundia, however, it was the beginning of an addiction.

Londe and Arendell had no objection when Delundia asked to move in with Ebbence. Both the dewy-eyed one-hander and the cagey old six-hander attested to the usefulness of their living together. For the sake of their work. And they did work.

Efficiency of the watermill went up sixteen percent. Delundia trained non-conductive coral to grow around and insulate several key lengths of wire in the town's watermill, and she convinced Ebbence that they should start designing a miniaturized version of the watermill engines that could be used to power individual households.

Meanwhile, Ebbence was living in a hazy dream of sex and affection. Despite his age, he can perhaps be forgiven for neglecting to realize how quickly Delundia's second birthing time was approaching. It had been so long since his own birthing times... Her parents, of course, assumed that with a genius like Ebbence to guide her, Delundia could do no wrong. Furthermore, they had thought Ebbence and Delundia were living together as mentor and apprentice—not husband and wife. So, they were as surprised as she was by the choice that was unwittingly made for her: Delundia's second birthing was a baby.

In the fluster of confusion that followed, Londe and Arendell insisted that the two lovers marry. Ebbence was not opposed, and Delundia was far too exhausted and distraught by finding herself burdened with an unwanted baby to object.

The ceremony was small for Delundia had made no friends her own age, living so far from town and spending all her time with Ebbence. Perhaps if she'd spent her time gossiping with other one-handers instead of studying with Ebbence, she'd have been wiser when it came to her own body. As it was, Delundia had no idea that there was a connection between the passionate night-time activities she shared with her new husband and the infant who had stolen her visions of already being a two-hander away.

Delundia was disappointed. She'd been hoping for a second hand to help her on her work. Instead of finding her consciousness multiplied, she found herself crippled from working at all. Now, while Ebbence continued their work, Delundia's one hand had to stay in the nursery that he quickly built for her and care for the baby whom they named Ata.

Delundia would not be daunted however, and she took to taking long walks around the surrounding hills, focusing all her efforts on developing the powerful control of her hand that Ebbence had over his. If she could not have multiple hands to control, she could at least learn masterful, long-distance control over her one hand.

Meanwhile, Ebbence found he'd fallen even deeper in love. Since all six of his births had been unfertilized hands, Ebbence had never had a child before, and he hadn't expected how it would affect him. He took to spending his days in the nursery, cooing at the baby and growing increasingly irritable with Delundia's carelessness.

"You lost hold of Ata twice today!" he scolded Delundia one evening when her main body came home. "If I hadn't been here, the currents would have carried her right out the door!"

Exhausted from hours of exertion, Delundia broke into sobs. Her hand secured the sleeping Ata snuggly into a swaddling net as carefully as possible, and then drew against her main body. Clutching against herself and heaving with sobs, Delundia couldn't understand how Ebbence managed to control his own hands from the other side of her father's farm. It was so much easier to control herself when her hand and body were near each other...

Ebbence convinced Delundia to give up the endeavor and stay near her hand until their child was older. With five hands worth of skilled caresses (while his sixth hand watched the baby), Ebbence soothed his young wife, promising that she could rejoin him in their work later.

Ata was a cheerful baby, and Delundia couldn't stay disappointed in her for long. She did wish for a second hand, but she didn't complain. Londe never bemoaned having too few hands, and Ebbence, who was clearly delighted with Ata, never expressed regret that luck had dealt him a life with no children of his own. So, Delundia tried to be as stoic as them. As the time of Delundia's third birthing approached, in fact, Delundia came to feel grateful for her experience of hardship. She was sure it had fortified her.

Nonetheless, she was more than ready for a second hand, and she delighted in her own awkward pudginess as her main body thickened. It was unusual for a one-hander to have birthed a baby, so she felt it was reasonable that she'd been disappointed. However, it was nearly unheard of for a one-hander to birth two babies, so she was sure this next birth would be the second hand she longed for. When the labor came, she hardly experienced the hours of excruciating pain. She was too focused on the expansion of her mind that would happen afterward.

So, it was with extreme confusion and a horrified wail that Delundia was presented with... another baby.

"How could this happen?!" she cried. "Why? Why?"

Londe clucked and tutted. "Now, now, your baby's perfect. Nothing's wrong."

Arendell, however, understood, and was horrified to realize that his brilliant daughter who could harness the quasi-magical power of electricity was still ignorant of the most basic facts about hand-haver life. He wanted to whisper to her the secret that he had failed her by not passing on earlier: to birth hands, abstain; to birth babies, make love. But he looked at his cherished Delundia—a burdened young mother with two babies to her one hand. He hadn't the resources to help her himself. She needed Ebbence. And Ebbence, who surely knew the truth of the difference between hands and babies, had not told his wife about it.

Had Ebbence made that choice for Delundia on purpose? Would Ebbence leave Delundia if she refused to have his children now? Arendell couldn't be sure. He couldn't think poorly of his old friend. Yet... He played it safe, and whispered to his daughter only the words, "Ebbence will care for you."

And he did care for her. If anything, Ebbence grew sweeter

and more solicitous. He devoted one hand to helping with the babies full-time, and Delundia, while disappointed in her lot, stayed as much in love with her wise, older lover as she ever had been. She never would have suspected that his love was the seed of her disaster... Until the day that Ebbence told her it himself.

Their first-born, Ata was a sprightly new one-hand, flitting about and enjoying her new duality. Watching her daughter made Delundia's regrets all the more painful. While Ata had birthed her first hand, Delundia had birthed yet another baby and had begun to wonder if there was something wrong with her. Three births older than her daughter, Delundia had no more hands than her and felt deeply ashamed. Instead of being the capable two- or three-hander she had expected to be at this age, she found herself with only two births left, once again nursing two no-handed infants with her single hand.

"I hope Ata's like you," Delundia said, wishing for her daughter what she could never have for herself.

Ebbence rotated his body, looking at his wife with his full concentricity of eyes. "A scientist?" he asked.

"A six-hander," she said.

"If she chooses that," he said, puffing his stubby body, "I would be very proud."

"Chooses?" Delundia asked.

"Of course," Ebbence said. One of his hands—the one that helped in the nursery—came to his wife and caressed her affectionately. "I have been extremely gratified," he said, "That your love for me is so great that you've never abstained from it, choosing to forego extra hands and stay a one-hander. It is an immensely flattering sacrifice."

Delundia was furious now that she finally understood.

The screaming and shouting of their fight carried through the water all the way to Londe and Arendell's house. Delundia's parents were not surprised when she came to them, carrying one baby in her own hand and followed by Ata who'd been conscripted to carry the other.

"Ebbence is your husband," Arendell said after Delundia made her case, begging them to let her stay with them. "The father of our grandchildren. And our oldest friend. He's been your mentor and your caretaker. We couldn't hurt him, 'Lundia."

"And how can you think of taking away Ata's youth with your own selfishness!" Londe added, coddling her grandchild. "Ata will stay with us. But you have to go."

Arendell and one of his hands helped his oldest birth-child carry her no-handed infants back to Ebbence's estate. "Make up with Ebbence," he begged as he left her. "I'm sure he'll forgive you."

Returned to her cage, Delundia swore that while she could not afford to leave Ebbence, she would never again love him. She banished his main body from the nursery and spent isolated days alone with the babies and the one hand Ebbence spent on helping her. It was utterly disheartening, but Delundia staked all her hopes on the day when her fifth birth would finally bring her a second hand of her own. That thought carried her, and, when her body finally started to thicken again, Delundia began to have a small glimmer of hope for her future. She'd never be the six-hander she'd dreamed of as a child... Or even a four-hander... But, she could yet be a three-hander like her father.

Then Ebbence came to her in the night.

Delundia awoke with her triad of hearts pounding. Her concentricity of mouths screamed, but Ebbence held her down with three hands. He begged her to see reason. He couldn't think straight without her. This rift between them was affecting his work, and he needed to feel her love again. His fourth hand wrestled her own hand into ineffectuality, and his final two hands watched the babies. He pressed against her; merged with her; all the while murmuring his love for her and how he knew she couldn't truly begrudge this liberty if she knew how much he needed her. It would be better for the both of them. Better for their work if he could concentrate. Better in the long run. When he left, Delundia sobbed until the morning.

Her fifth birth was a baby.

Ironically, for the first time, Delundia was not disappointed. For once, she'd known before the birth that it would, in fact, be a baby and not a hand. She knew, finally, that it wasn't her poor luck to blame. It wasn't the baby's fault.

It was Ebbence. And what he'd done to her. Delundia felt as if her soul would burn out consuming her inside a chasm of grief and anger.

Isolated as she was, Delundia took an ironic comfort in her new child, Qyio. All the adults in her life—Ebbence, Arendell, Londe, and her two one-handed children—avoided Delundia. No one spoke to her. One of Ebbence's hands watched the older infant, but Delundia kept Qyio for herself. At first, she meant to murder this infant, product of rape. The life she'd wanted was gone. The person she'd wanted to be... Eradicated. Stolen away, piece by piece, as her body had treacherously transformed unborn hands—her hands—into unwanted children.

Yet the only solace she found was in the cooing bundle of infancy that she cradled between her body and hand. Qyio was less hers than a hand would have been... But still hers. A spark lit Qyio's infant body with a life both foreign and achingly familiar. The cerulean tinge of Qyio's flesh was wholly Ebbence, but the pudgy curve around Qyio's eyes was her.

To kill Qyio would be to darken the only light in her life. She might as well kill herself.

Instead, Delundia grew numb. Passing through her life as though she were only hands—dumb, mindless, with no sentient body in control.

In this state, Ebbence finally came to her.

"I miss my 'Lundia," he said.

She did not answer.

"Our work together has been so beautiful."

Delundia's body quaked. Perhaps she was laughing. Perhaps she was sobbing. She didn't know.

"The miniaturized watermills we designed together power every house in the village." Ebbence's pudgy body gestured expansively with nubby limbs. "And our children..."

Delundia's concentricity of eyes contorted to focus fiercely on Ebbence as she listened to what he had to say.

"Our children are the greatest part of all."

More than anything in the world, Delundia would have wanted to go back to the beginning and save herself the mistakes that brought her to where she was... But she could not have that. She would never be the six-hander self that she could wistfully, heartbreakingly imagine.

Yet, she could be a mother who believed her children had been a worthwhile contribution. She could believe, if she tried hard enough... She could believe that she wanted the children.

Ebbence offered her that. And to the horror of the sliver of herself left over that still dreamed of all the great things a six-handed Delundia could have done, she gave herself to him.

Delundia chose love and submission. And passion.

Setting Qyio safely aside in a swaddling net, Delundia's hand grasped Ebbence to her. The press of his body against hers, after so long, was electric. Before his hands could even leave their workshop to join them, the last fleeting hope of Delundia ever birthing another hand of her own passed away in a gasp of consummation. She would be one-handed forever.

At the venerable age of six-births, Delundia was a one-handed mother of five children. Despite her relative disability, Delundia never wanted for anything, materially. Her six-handed husband saw to that until the day he died—not long after their fifth and final child entered one-handed adolescence.

As Delundia resigned herself to her position in life, her other family members returned to her. Londe congratulated her on her wisdom and self-restraint: "What good does an extra hand do you," she asked, "if you clearly don't need one?" Londe scolded her husband for his short-sightedness. Why, they could have had another two or three children between them if they'd only worked harder and skimped more. Like Delundia. Instead, they were left in old age with all these useless hands rattling about.

Arendell stayed silent. He'd missed his chance to say his part when Delundia was young and a few instructive words from him could have made a difference.

For her part, Delundia saw to it that each of her own children were acquainted with all the facts, and she made it her personal mission to ensure that every one of them birthed at least three hands. They teased her for her hypocrisy—birthing only one hand herself and insisting they behave differently. But Delundia cajoled, pleaded, and reasoned.

Four of her five children folded easily. Ata put up the only real fight, having spent so many of her formative one-hand years being raised by Londe. In the end, however, Delundia won. Ata chose to appease her silly one-handed mother, and Delundia was delighted to see her daughter's competence and consciousness expand upon birthing her third hand. It was a vicarious pleasure.

The greatest happiness Delundia ever knew, though, was when Qyio came to her near the end. While his siblings saw the silly one-hander that Delundia had chosen to be when life gave her no other choice, Qyio knew the broken-hearted six-hander that she kept buried deep inside. "I'll continue your work," he promised her, for Delundia had continued planning and designing, even without the hands to carry out her plans, to build her designs.

"I'll string wires, coated in coral between every house in the village, creating a network of interconnected electronic signals..." He described to Delundia her own dream for the future of their village, a veritable technopticon of communication and convenience.

Delundia smiled with half of her mouths, thinking of the world she could have lived in if she'd only had the hands necessary to build it for herself. But then there would be no Qyio, and she couldn't have that. He was so much like her, so much the person she'd wanted to be. She died loving her son and also regretting him.

21

FOREKNOWLEDGE

I stare out over my pregnant belly, feeling awkward. Feeling irritable. "Why wouldn't I want to know?"

"Some parents don't want to know," Dr. Anders says. "And we respect that."

"It's right there on your clipboard, right?" I point to the clipboard, and he holds it infinitesimally closer to his chest. As if he's hiding the results from me.

"Yes," Dr. Anders says. "Both the sex and cause of death of your unborn child are right here."

"Isn't it kind of artificial then?" I ask. "I mean, you and all the nurses will just keep looking at that clipboard every week when we come in. So, you'd have to purposely conceal it from us."

"Yes," Dr. Anders says. "But we're happy to do that."

He smiles, and it strikes me wrong.

"Tell you what," he says, folding the clipboard under his arm. "I'll give you two a minute to talk it over."

Dr. Anders leaves me and my husband Chad in the hospital exam room, closing the door behind him. I don't want a minute to think about it. I don't want to spend any extra time wearing a paper gown.

"Do you get the sense that he doesn't want to tell us?" Chad says.

I frown. "I don't see why he wouldn't."

The more I know about this baby, the sooner I can start to feel attached to it. I know some women bond with their babies before they're born… So far, though, the only time I've felt any love for the parasite inside me is when we did the ultrasound. The images were grainy and hard to understand, but they were images of a person. Most of the time, this baby is just a twisty lump inside my belly that feels more like a squirming alien tumor than a tiny human being.

"I don't know," Chad says. "I mean, we've all heard the horror stories. Like the new parents who found out their baby boy's cause of death would be SISTER."

"Right, except, that won't be a problem for us," I say, shifting my weight uncomfortably. "Because we've already decided that we're having an only child, right?" I give Chad a meaningful look, and he nods. I don't ever want to be pregnant again. If Chad could have babies, I wouldn't have agreed to be pregnant this time.

"Of course," Chad says, "just to play devil's advocate here, you do know that those parents decided not to have another child, too?"

I glare at Chad in a way that lets him know this might not be the best time for playing devil's advocate. Besides, I've heard this story before, so I do know that. I also know how it ends. "He was in a coma," I say. "Someone had to pull the plug on his life support."

"Even so," Chad says, "it must have been hard for the parents. Watching their baby daughter, worrying about how she'd someday be the death of their son."

"Any story is a horror story if you focus on the right parts of it," I say.

Chad is still looking at me, expecting me to argue with him about this piece of urban mytho-history. I don't want to argue.

"I want to know," I say, losing my patience.

"Okay," Chad says, rubbing my shoulder affectionately. He's not really worried about this. If he were, we'd have talked about it before. He just likes to cover all his bases. Think everything through carefully. It's a good trait. Sometimes.

Dr. Anders finally returns and says, "All right, then. Is there anything we need to talk about before scheduling your next appointment? Questions about exercise? Anything like that?"

Maybe Chad is right. Maybe Dr. Anders doesn't want to tell us. Chad and I look at each other, and then Chad says, "We want to know the sex and cause of death." His words are definite. There's no uncertainty.

Dr. Anders nods slowly. "Your baby is a girl," he says.

That was my secret hope, and my heart leaps at the sudden image, vague but glowing, that fills my eyes. Taking my daughter to the park, brushing her hair, picking out ruffled dresses, and playing with dolls. I don't know her hair or eye color, the shape of her face, the turn of her nose... But she has become infinitely more real for me. "Amanda," I breathe. This is the name that Chad and I picked out. I place my hands on my belly. Now I know who's in there. "Amanda." I feel much better. I can't wait to learn more about her.

"And," Dr. Anders says, "she'll die from SIDS."

"What?" I say. His words don't make sense.

"Sudden Infant Death Syndrome."

Chad asks, "The thing where babies stop breathing and die for no discernable reason?"

The world has closed in around my ears. Everything sounds like an echo chamber, but they're still talking. I'm missing important information. "What did you say?" I ask, trying to understand this situation.

"Before the age of one," Dr. Anders repeats.

"That's... very young," Chad says.

"I'm afraid so," Dr. Anders agrees. "But, as I'm sure you know, these predictions are notoriously misleading."

Chad frowns, but I can see he's trying to listen. Trying as hard as I am. "How could... SIDS be misleading?" Chad asks.

"Well, um, off the top of my head," Dr. Anders says, "It could mean that your daughter will one day... um... have a baby of her own who dies from SIDS... and then... um... kill herself?"

"That's not better," Chad says, his voice flat.

Except, of course, it is. This year, right now, it's better. Any interpretation that means our daughter won't die this year is better.

The rest of the appointment passes in a somber hush, which is just as well, because the world still feels like an echo chamber to me. All those images of my daughter and the great life we'll have together just stop now. Before the age of one. The rest of my life stretches before my eyes in painful, isolated, desolation. My life right now is before Amanda. In a little over a year, my life will become after Amanda. It would be better not to have her at all.

"What about an abortion?" I ask as we're getting in the car to drive home.

Chad shakes his head. We both know it's too late in the pregnancy. No doctor would perform one. Besides, my daughter doesn't die from ABORTION. She dies from SIDS.

I SORT THROUGH THE boxes of baby clothes that our parents have given us. Amanda will be the first grandchild on both sides, so we get all the hand-me-downs. Our parents are all very excited. We haven't told them about Amanda's death prediction. They assume it's something normal, something cryptic. Maybe it is?

The clothes in the box from Chad's parents are funny. A little black velvet vest, red coveralls, tiny shirts with tiny blue sailboats on them. I try to picture Chad wearing them as a baby.

The box from my parents is full of memories. Thinking about dressing Amanda in them feels like a return to my own childhood. Life is circular.

Without thinking about it too clearly, I sort all the clothes into two piles: larger than 12M and smaller than 12M. I fold the bigger ones back into the boxes. The smaller ones go into the drawers under Amanda's crib.

She could be born any day now, and we have to be ready.

❧

THE LABOR PAINS START.

❧

IT'S BEEN HOURS, and I can't believe it's possible to hurt this much. How can I feel this much pain without dying?

❧

MY DAUGHTER IS HANDED to me. Her body is warm, and red, and squishy. I know what heaven feels like. It lies on the other side of hell. It feels like holding Amanda in my arms.

❧

It's time to leave the hospital. Amanda is in my arms, and Chad wheels our chair to the elevator. Part of me doesn't want to look at her. I know she's going to leave me, and I need to pull my heart away before she does.

The doors to the elevator open, and Chad wheels us into the hospital lobby. It's a long room, running the whole length of the hospital, with two-story windows above all the automatic doors to the outside. People come and go. It's busy today.

I see Amanda's eyes widen: this is the first time she's seen anything other than the floor of the hospital she was born on. Her entire world has multiplied magnificently. She had no idea, moments ago in the elevator, that the universe was this large and interesting.

I feel my heart swell with love for her like a balloon swelling into the tip of a knife.

EVERY NIGHT, I burst into tears when Chad says it's time to put Amanda down in her crib. We fight for a few minutes, sometimes longer, and then Chad gives in. Amanda sleeps in our bed, next to me. I listen to her breathe all night. Treasuring each moment. Getting more tired every day.

I stare at her in the dim light of our bedroom at night, imagining all the ways we might have misunderstood SIDS. She could be a babysitter someday—a very old woman who has outlived me—and she'll be murdered by the angry father of an infant who died on her watch. She could have a heart attack— as a very, very old woman—when she discovers that one of her great, great grandchildren has suffered from SIDS and died in her arms. She could be on an airplane—enjoying some travel during her retirement years—when the pilot is told his infant at home has died from SIDS. Frantic with grief, the pilot plummets the ship down, down to a horrible watery crash in the middle of the ocean.

My thoughts are insane and loopy, they share three trends. No matter how far from reality I stray, Amanda grows to be a very, very old woman; the infant who suffers a sudden death is not one I currently know—certainly not the precious baby Amanda now sleeping in my arms; and none of them make much sense. But, then, neither does a world like this. Miserable, wretched world. The only sense is Amanda.

Every breath she takes is perfect. The curve of her cheeks; the thin, lightly closed eyelids; the little sighs she makes. I can't imagine doing anything but watch her breathe. For the rest of my life. For the rest of her life.

I think... As unthinkable as it sounds, I'm waiting for her to stop. Then I can move on.

~

AMANDA IS SEVEN MONTHS OLD, and Chad's finally convinced me that she should sleep in her crib at night. I wouldn't have agreed, but Amanda's getting bigger. The doctor says that most cases of SIDS happen in the first six months. Most. Not all. Besides, she's taken to thrashing her arms about in her sleep, wanting her own space. No one gets any sleep with her in the bed with us.

I lay in Chad's arms, feel the weight of his body above mine when we make love, and I feel no magic in his touch. The only magic in the whole world is held in that tiny body in the quiet room across the hall. No matter how I strain, I cannot hear her breathing, and, every night, I'm sure will be her last.

~

AMANDA IS TEN MONTHS OLD, and we've taken her to the park. We've laid out a blanket on the grass, and we're having a picnic for Valentine's Day. There's fried chicken, greasy on our fingers, for Chad and me. Amanda gums away at a mushy mix of vegetables.

"Should we plan a birthday party?" Chad says, putting his chicken bones back in the grease-stained paper bag.

"A birthday party?" I ask.

"For Amanda," he says. "My parents always did big family, barbecue, get-together things for my birthday when I was a little kid."

I stare at him blankly. "April isn't a really good time for that," I say, wanting this conversation to go away. "It'll be too cold for a barbecue."

Chad looks at me strangely. "Okay," he says.

"What?" I say, accusation in my voice. I'm not sure what I'm accusing him of, but I'm angry anyway.

Chad shrugs, and we sit on the blanket together in unhappy silence. Amanda loses interest in her vegetable smoosh and looks about for a new entertainment. Her movements are wobbly, unpracticed. She sees the playground behind us, bright with colorful plastic play structures, and she bats an arm, as if she could grab that far away object without moving toward it. With a frown of concentration, Amanda leans into a crawl and pushes herself upward. She wants to walk, but she's never succeeded before.

A wobble, a fall. Another try, and she takes a step. I gasp, and Chad grabs my arm. "She's walking!" he says. I say, "I see it! I see it!"

All in all, she only takes five steps toward the playground before plopping back on her bum. She cries at the unfairness of a universe where such a pretty sight is placed out of her reach. I can fix that problem for her, and I swing her up in my arms. I carry her to the playground, place her in a swing, and listen to the happy laughter of a baby flying through the air as I give her gentle pushes.

I can't fix my own problem, though. After ten months of treasuring every second—trying to treasure every second; every single second—I am tired. I want to move on.

Chad comes up behind me and says, "If you won't plan a birthday party, maybe we should start making other plans."

"What do you mean?" I say, but I'm afraid I do know.

"We could go to Hawaii for our anniversary this year," he says. "We'd need to book tickets ahead of time though."

Part of me likes that idea, but I say, "It sounds like a lot of work to take a baby to Hawaii, and I don't know that Amanda will be weaned yet. She might still be nursing."

We both know that she won't be nursing. She'd be fifteen months old. She's never going to be fifteen months old.

I stop the swing and pull Amanda out of the baby seat, against her protestations. I hold her in my arms and think how new the world is to her. She's just begun to walk, and she'll never learn to swim or dance or drive a car. She'll never learn how to cartwheel or somersault. I may never hear her talk. "I can't plan anything right now," I say.

"We have to plan something," Chad says, "or I don't know what will happen when... What will happen..." He balls his hands into fists. "I don't know how we're going to make it through this!"

"What are you saying?" I ask, thinking about how distant I've been. How frustrating life with me must be for Chad. "Is that some sort of threat? When... I mean... Are you saying you're going to leave... us..."

The word—the one that means me and Amanda—hangs in the air between me and Chad. We both know how temporary it is. What I'm really asking is whether he'll leave me. Alone with the empty space where I now hold the warm, impatient, inarticulate body of my daughter. I carry Amanda back to the blanket with our picnic and set her down. She grabs a shiny rattle and starts beating against the crinkly bag of leftover chicken bones, punctuating each beat with an indecipherable nonsense syllable.

When I turn back to Chad, I see his face contorted by tears. He never cries. I'm scared that maybe he really does plan to leave me. We won't be a family any more when Amanda dies. Just two sad people. And if I thought I was never willing to go through pregnancy a second time before, I know for sure that I could never, ever go through it again now. I couldn't face that uncertainty.

That's it. He'll leave. Chad has always wanted to be a father. He argued with me for years before agreeing that one child would be enough. He'd never consent to none.

He'll find another woman. And he'll have his family. I'll have the ghost of him and the searing, burning gash on my heart left by Amanda.

"I would never leave you," Chad says. "But, I know you. And if we don't make plans, you're going to... It won't be good when... I mean... God! How can we even talk about this?" He's actually asking, truly confused.

I put my hands out to him, and he buries his face in the curve of my shoulder.

His voice is muffled against me: "If I didn't know for a fact that your death ticket says OLD AGE," he says, "I'd think for sure that you'd kill yourself. You'd leave me."

"I wish I could," I say. I'd always loved that death prediction. I felt so lucky. I don't feel lucky anymore.

I feel Chad's body wrack with sobs against mine. I start crying too.

"Please don't," he says. "I know that she's your whole world." He tightens his arms around me until it hurts. "But you're mine. Please don't go."

I can't, I think. I couldn't kill myself if I wanted to. But, he means: don't leave him. And I can't promise that right now. I can't promise anything. I can't give him even that much. Even if it means pushing him further away. Maybe I want to push him away. Maybe it will be better if we end up apart. Instead of pulling each other down, drowning together in our pain.

"I can't make plans," I say. "I just can't. Not yet."

Chad nods. His head is still pressed into my shoulder. He says, "Fine." A minute later, he whispers, "But I have to."

I run my fingers through his hair until he manages to hide the last of his tears away. We pack the picnic up and go home in silence. Amanda takes another five steps before we put her to bed that night, and as I close the door to her room I worry about what kind of plans Chad might make.

I'M COUNTING the days now. Some mornings, I run into her room as fast as I can, needing to know, instantly, whether today is the day. The horrible day.

Other mornings, I can't stand it. I really, really can't stand the idea of walking into her room and finding her in her crib. Cold and blue. I wait by her door on those mornings, crying until I hear her cry.

If she doesn't cry one of those mornings, will I wait by her door all day? Will she lie there dead all day?

I can't take it. I cannot take it.

AMANDA'S BIRTHDAY is in a week.

I've decided that we can't have made it this close and then not make it. Her death card can't really mean that she'll die from SIDS. Not simply. Not directly. Our family is going to be one of those stories. The funny stories about how death predictions are always true, but never really mean what you think they will.

~

OH GOD, oh god, oh god, oh god.

~

SHE'S GONE.

~

CHAD WASN'T LYING when he said he'd make plans. He planned the whole funeral. The birthday too. So we'd be ready either way, he says.

~

THOSE HOURS before Amanda was born were hell. I didn't know a human body could experience that much pain, but I would live there forever, existing always in those moments of physical torture wracking my entire body, if I could only be that close to her again.

~

THE DAYS STRETCH ON, and the pain doesn't kill me. I don't understand why it doesn't.

Amanda would be fifteen months old now. I look up baby classes I could sign her up for online.

The webpages are cheerful with colorful fonts and happy pictures. There's a music class where babies play with tambourines and xylophones while their mothers sit in a circle watching them. A gymnastics class where babies tumble about on a foam mat, trying to crawl over stair steps and through hula hoops. The mothers smile and clap, encouraging their children. Hoping their babies will turn out to be Olympians earning gold medals or tiny Mozarts writing concertos. Fantasies. And when the fantasies melt away, those mothers have their plain, ordinary children, alive in their arms. Graduating from second tier colleges. Getting crummy jobs. But alive.

That will not be my life.

I don't know what my life will be, but it will be empty.

I'm at the park where Amanda took her first steps. There are children playing, and I try to imagine Amanda among them. She's a phantom on the swings, riding the merry-go-round, and stabbing a little yellow shovel into the sand.

There's a girl who looks to be about Amanda's age. Lighter hair. A little chubbier. Smiling. I wonder if they would have been friends. They'd play together, and I'd strike up a conversation with the other little girl's mother.

I wonder what the girl's death card reads. Probably OLD AGE like mine. I hate her. And her mother.

I see Chad's car pull into the parking lot. He gets out of the car, and I can tell he's looking for me, standing in the open car door. But I don't wave. I don't call out. When he sees me, he looks relieved and maybe angry too. He gets back in the car, and I think he'll drive away. Instead, he gets back out with a folder tucked under his arm.

My heart grows cold. Those will be the divorce papers. He told me he'd be making plans, and I've done nothing to stop him. I still love him. I don't want him to leave me, but I don't have it in me to stop him. Even if all that means is asking him not to go.

Chad sits down on the park bench beside me. "I've been looking everywhere for you," he says.

He looks at me, and I look at the children. I won't look at him, and he can't look at them. I've noticed that. Since Amanda died, he turns away whenever there's a baby. Especially little girls. With dark hair and soulful eyes. I start to cry.

"We can't go on like this forever," he says.

I bite my lip, stifle the tears. I'm getting better at that. Though they're still inside.

"Look, I know you're probably not ready for this now, but, I've been talking to... Well... Here, just look at this." He hands me the folder.

At first, I won't take it, but he folds my hands around it. He moves my hands like I'm a puppet, making me open the folder. But I don't look down.

"I want to have a family," he says.

"I won't have another baby." It's a reflex. I think those words all the time. Arguing with myself, I'll think, it might be better a second time. The death prediction would be different. Holding a second infant in my arms would be a happy experience, not one wracked with guilt and terror. Not a betrayal of Amanda.

But I don't believe any of it. And I know I'll never change my mind.

Chad sounds frustrated, and he gets up to leave. "Just... look at the third packet," he says. "Okay?" He turns away, walks to the car, and gets in. But he doesn't drive away. He's waiting for me.

I look down at the folder, and I see something I didn't expect. There's a blue sheet of information on becoming adoptive parents, followed by packets of information about foster children in the area.

The child in the third packet is a four-year-old girl. Her face in the picture paperclipped to the pages of information is unremarkable. Gaunt, haunted blue eyes, nothing like Amanda who'd been hardy and healthy. For every day she had. Then I read this foster child's death prediction: CHILDHOOD LEUKEMIA. She was born with it.

Like Amanda, she's going to die. A child. Her parents are already dead, and there's no one who'd willingly sign on for that kind of pain.

Almost no one. Chad and I have practice with it.

And, suddenly, in those blue eyes, cursed with the same horrible fate as my own dead and buried baby, I see Amanda's sister. I see Amanda.

22

HEAVEN IS THE BEST MOMENT OF
YOUR LIFE, INFINITELY REMIXED
AND PLAYED ON LOOP

When I was a kid, cryogenically freezing yourself was something crazy rich people with more money and desperation to live forever than actual common sense did to themselves to escape dying. It was a joke. And I can't entirely get over seeing it that way.

And yet, here I am.

I put my daughter in charge of my finances years ago, and she assures me this is affordable and works. She's good with numbers and research, like her dad was. I've always been the impulsive one. The artist. She's more grounded, and nonetheless, she says a lot of people have come out of cryogenic freezes lately. While it all sounds a bit hokey to me, I have to admit, it's easier to accept than the idea of dying from this damned disease before the scientists finish testing and double-testing the damned cure. I just need to make it a few more years without dying, and then I can have another twenty or more.

So, if that means letting my daughter pay a bunch of entrepreneurs to freeze me for a little while, I guess I'll trust her and play along.

"Come on, Mom," Haley stands up from the chairs we've

been waiting in, gesturing toward a woman standing in an open door. "The guidance counselor is ready for us."

"Guidance counselor?" I ask. "What am I back in high school?" I chuckle at my own joke, but Haley just shakes her head and leads the way into an office decorated in different shades of white, extremely minimalist.

We sit down at the one desk, and the woman, who's now sitting behind it smiles. She's dressed in a white suit to match the room, like an angel in a 1980s movie's depiction of heaven, where everyone stands in orderly lines, waiting to be reincarnated.

"Hello, you must be Dani," the woman says. "Your daughter's told me all about your case. We've already gone over the administrative and legal side. All I need from you before we can proceed is to select the mix of moments that you want to build your personal heaven from."

I look at Haley uncertainly. The roundness in her cheeks when she smiles encouragingly back at me makes me think of Marty, like it always does, no matter how many years he's been gone.

"It's very simple," the woman dressed in white says, proceeding in spite of my clear hesitation. Though, I think she's made her tone softer in deference to it. "We do a quick brain scan, and our proprietary AI will select a dozen or so of the moments when you were happiest. We'll agree on two or three of them—we've found it's best if we keep the dreamscape simple—and then while you're frozen, we'll keep your brain stimulated, causing it to form an endless dream centered on those seed memories. You'll create your own slice of heaven for yourself while you sleep, waiting for us to unfreeze you and wake you up again."

The woman smiles. It's the smile of an actor at the end of a commercial when they hold up the product they want you to buy.

But Haley reaches over and squeezes my arm. Her smile is real. "Doesn't that sound great? A few years of dreaming, and then I can have you back again. And I'll catch you up on everything you missed!"

Now I smile too. I like that idea. I want to survive to make it into the future and see how much my daughter can accomplish, and see how her son, my young grandson, turns out. I have more things I want to accomplish too. I always told Marty I would write a book someday—something longer than my poetry. Maybe a graphic novel, combining words with my drawings. And right now, if I still want to believe in that dream, I have a choice—I can buckle down and try to write a book while getting sicker and sicker, racing against time. Or I can do what my daughter's told me to do, and let this corporate idea of an angel scan my brain.

"Okay," I say. "Whatever you need to do, let's do it."

The woman in white beams at me, opens a desk drawer, pulls out a simple headset, and hands it across the desk to me. "Just put this on, and we can get right to work designing heaven for you." Now she turns to my daughter. "Haley, why don't give your mother and I some privacy? I can have her back to you in an hour so, and then we can schedule the freezing for early next week."

Haley's brow wrinkles. She wants to stay. She's paying for it, and it's her idea. She'll have to spend years waiting for me to come back, while I take the short road of falling asleep, dreaming awhile, and waking up like no time has passed. It does seem only fair that she should get to see what I'm dreaming about. Except...

"Uh... when you say 'happiest,'" I begin to ask, putting air quotes around the final word, "what exactly do you mean?"

"Oh!" the woman in white exclaims. "No, no, we won't be selecting any memories of a—uh, shall we say—more physically intimate nature. Our research shows that they don't play nicely with the cryogenic state we need to keep our clients' bodies in. We're looking more for memories that involve a state of euphoric, peaceful joy. True, pure happiness, plain and simple." Again, that smile straight from the end of a cereal commercial.

Do they still advertise cereal? I don't even know. I've paid to keep every form of media I imbibe clean of advertising—except the really targeted ads that are for things I'll actually enjoy—for years now.

"Great," I say, fidgeting with the headset in my hands, "then I see no reason why Haley can't stay and help me choose what I'll be dreaming about."

The woman in white looks uncomfortable. "This can be a very personal process…"

"My daughter and I are very close," I say, and I'm rewarded with a smug grin from Haley—the same one I remember on her face when she was five and would convince me to let her have dessert for breakfast. I love that grin. It makes me feel like we're co-conspirators, not just parent and child.

The woman in white shrugs and explains how to properly fit the headset behind my ears and across my forehead. It has sucker discs that Haley helps me affix properly. When the woman in white activates it, the headset hums warmly on my brow.

The woman picks up a computer tablet, swipes her fingers across the screen a few times, nods to herself, and then says, "There are some definite peaks that standout. Shall we start looking at them?"

I say something that comes out as a confusing hybrid of "sure" and "okay," at the same time as Haley announces, without any hesitation, "Absolutely!"

The woman turns the tablet towards us, and there's some kind of graph on it, showing peaks and dips. It makes me think of a seismographic chart or the readout from a lie detector test.

The woman flicks her fingers, zooming in on part of the chart, and then taps on a tall spike. Suddenly, the chart is replaced with hazy imagery of me sitting on a couch. An old, beat-up yellow couch.

"I remember that couch!" I say. "Martin and I found it at a thrift store. It's the most comfortable couch we ever had, and I've always regretted that we didn't get a U-Haul and bring it with us when we moved."

Haley's brow has furrowed again. "You're just sitting on a couch, Mom. What's going on here?" She looks quizzically at the woman in white. "Are you sure you're using that thing right?"

"This memory is definitely a significant peak in your happiness timeline, Dani." The woman in white is making a definite point of looking at me, and not my daughter.

"We still had that couch when you born," I tell Haley. "We used to nap on it together when you were a baby. In fact, based on the rest of the decoration in the room, you'd have been a few years old in this memory." I stare at the image a little longer and realize that the important part of the memory isn't the couch—it's what's on the television screen.

At the same time as my realization, Haley asks, "What's that you're watching on TV?"

"Uh..." I feel my cheeks burn bright red.

"Is that Yessica Casper onscreen?"

I can feel Haley's gaze peering into the private side of my past. I hadn't realized I had any secrets from her, not really. And I guess, it's not really much of a secret. It's too silly to be a real secret. "Yes," I say. "I was watching this lawyer show. It was okay, nothing special. But then, one week, they did a musical episode and had Yessica Casper as a guest star. I'd never heard her music before. And you know I love musicals."

"Okay," Haley says, trying to make sense of this. "Yeah, okay,

I remember when we started watching all her movies and listening to her music. She was pretty good."

I shrug, trying to play it off as nothing. "Yeah, I liked her music. She's very, uh, talented."

I must have replayed her songs in that episode about a thousand times in a row when it first came out. I couldn't believe my eyes when the whole cast of the show started dancing around her, and her voice? I felt like I'd died and gone to heaven just listening to her.

So, I guess I shouldn't be surprised that it registered as such a huge happiness peak in my life. If Marty were still alive, he'd be laughing at me. He wouldn't be surprised. The crush I had on Yessica Casper bordered on actual love. Sure, I didn't know her, never would, but simply seeing her face could make me happy. Reading her song lyrics—the ones she wrote, because she was a damn good songwriter and wrote most of her own songs—made me feel like I was learning about what it meant to be alive. And watching her dance? It felt like my whole body turned to water—all wibbly and transparent. Like the brightness of her light could shine right through me.

Marty had never minded my celebrity crushes. He just played along and said he enjoyed the extra, shall we say, passion they incited. It was like a rollercoaster ride for both of us when my brain latched onto someone like Yessica. Just strap in and stay for the ride. Marty always liked rollercoasters better than I did.

For me, it felt like my brain had turned into a golden retriever, and videos of Yessica were its favorite ball—the dog ran off, refusing to come back, refusing to drop the ball, and I had to just keep thinking about Yessica and how perfect she was, thoughts of her dancing intruding in everything I did for weeks, until my idiot of a brain got tired and went back to normal.

I guess that's what falling in love feels like? It's not what it felt like with Marty. I loved my husband very much. He was my best friend, and I loved every year we spent together. We did everything together and told each other everything. But...

Well. There it was on the damned screen in this stranger's hands: the happiest I'd ever been in my life—a life with a husband and daughter I still loved—was the moment I'd first seen Yessica Casper and heard her sing. If that's not falling in love of some sort... Well, I don't know.

The woman in white walks me and Haley through several other peaks on my happiness timeline, and we talk about each of them in the same way as the first one. Ultimately, they're all similar—moments when something surprised and truly delighted me in a movie, television show, or music album I'd been anticipating. Haley's expression is getting weirder and weirder. Usually I can read her like a book, but right now, I don't what she's thinking. It makes me feel judged and small.

"I think our best bet is to simply go with these top three moments," the woman in white says, turning the computer tablet face down on her desk. She holds one of her hands out and says, "You can take the headset off now. We have everything we need."

"So... you'll... what?" Haley asks. "Build a heaven out of Yessica Casper singing on a lawyer show, sitting in a car listening to Yessica's first album for the first time, and whatever that thing with the doctor show was?"

"It was a crossover event episode," I say, handing the headset over to the woman in white. My words are dry, mechanical. But I remember the episode—two episodes of different shows, actually—and they were spectacular. It was the kind of episode that a pair of shows can only do when they've been on the air for decades and you've seen all the characters grow up from baby twenty-year-olds to confident adults in their fifties. You just can't tell the same kind of story with one-off characters who the audience has never seen before and will never see again. It takes history. The kind of history that simulates reality so well that, apparently, my brain can't tell the difference.

"That's pretty much the idea," the woman in white says, sounding serious, but it's more forced now than before. Less like a cereal commercial, and more like a parent telling their kid it's time to leave the playground while hoping the kid isn't going to throw a fit and embarrass them. But her expression softens suddenly, and she says, "Look, there's a reason I suggested you should leave for this process. These happiness charts don't always work the way people expect them to—I've built heaven out of a person watching a leaf fall onto the surface of a pond, playing fetch with their dog, and enjoying the warm sudsy feel of washing dishes. Washing dishes! Can you imagine? But the person in question felt content and peaceful during that moment. And that's the kind of feeling we're looking for. We need emotions that play nice with long term stasis."

Haley nods and quirks her mouth into an expression that manages to look like both a dissatisfied frown and a polite smile at the same time, like some kind of optical illusion of emotion. She thanks the woman in white, and the two of us leave the office. And the building.

When we're standing outside on the sidewalk in front, the leaves in the trees above move in the breeze, making the shadows and sunlight play over us. It makes me think of a heaven built out of falling leaves and dishwater.

"I'm sorry," I blurt out. "It should have been memories of you, when you were a baby. Maybe Marty's and my wedding day. Not... Yessica." And yet, I love her music so much—everything about her, really—that just saying Yessica's name, even all these years later, makes me happy. Again, if that's not a kind of love... I just don't know.

Haley shakes her head, squares her shoulders, and looks at

me straight on, expression serious. "You don't need to be sorry. It's your heaven. And... it's not like it changes how close we are. I just..." She smiles impishly and raises a single eyebrow. "I didn't realize Yessica Casper meant that much to you."

I shrug and sigh, like some kind of deflating balloon.

"I guess it makes sense, though," Haley says, mulling her thoughts over. Sometimes when I watch her while she's thinking, I can practically see the thoughts churning and turning over in her head. "When I was a baby, you were probably scared out of your mind for me. That's how I felt after Ryan was born."

"All the time," I agree. "Happy and terrified. And tired."

Her eyes brighten, and then cloud again just as quickly. "What about when Ryan was born? Meeting your grandchild?"

"Twice as terrified," I say. "Childbirth is dangerous, so I was scared for both you and him."

She nods somberly. A beat later, "And when you married Dad... that's like a whole thing, doing the old-style wedding with family. It was probably a lot of pressure?"

"Probably." I don't disagree. "Although, honestly..." I amend, "it's hard to remember. There was so much chaos on that day."

Haley's lips tighten and she nods. "Yeah, I can see that. And, like, when WWIII ended? I know it was only a few years long, but like, I've seen the videos of people dancing in the street all around the world. They were ecstatic!"

"Oh god, don't even get me started on that," I exclaim. And yet—too late—she got me started. "I was so torn up from the bad things that had been happening... and so convinced that the peace would be overturned before anything really settled down—"

"Okay, okay." Haley holds her hands up, palm forward, placating. "I get it. And I should know better than to bring up politics with you. That was never something that would make you happy. But... Yessica."

"Yeah, Yessica," I agree, shrugging again. "She's... perfect. At least, what I get to see of her. Polished, produced, and performed to perfection. There's nothing quite as perfect as a Yessica Casper music video."

"It's simple," Haley agrees. "Simple happiness."

"Yeah." I reach out and take my daughter's hand. "But it's not real life."

Now I get that smile I love so much again—the beaming one, the one that reminds me of Marty.

"So, I'll dream heaven for a few years, and then I'll come back to reality. Because that's where I'd rather be. And you'll catch me up on everything."

Now she gives me a mischievous smile that's all me—I've seen it in pictures; I've seen it in the mirror. It's the expression I make when I know I'm about to try to stir up some trouble. "Perhaps, especially the new Yessica Casper music videos," she says.

23

TWO ROADS DIVERGE

Sometimes two roads diverge in a wood, and you can never know what would have happened if you'd taken the other path. Or so I'm told. It hasn't been that way since before I was born.

Like my mother before me, I lay my hand on the hypercrystal when it's time to decide what I want to do with my life—whether I want to have a child and become a mother or... not.

People use the hypercrystals for all sorts of reasons, of course. Not just big decisions, like this one.

I've used the hypercrystal to decide what I want to eat for breakfast, what book to read next, or even if I should get up off my lazy ass and go to bed or keep bingeing whatever sitcom I'm hooked on at the moment.

Spoiler: the hypercrystal ALWAYS tells me to go to bed; the future where I do that is ALWAYS, ALWAYS the better one. Big surprise. And even bigger surprise—only about half the time do I do what it says. The other half, I fall asleep on the couch and wake up to a sore neck and stiff back. It's never worth it. Just like the hypercrystal said. But people can be stupid that way.

Today though, I need to really decide. I need to decide because I can't stand worrying and dithering over this choice any longer, and I just need to know—should I push the button on the mechano-womb to start the incubation process or... not?

The crystal's warm under my hand as I close my eyes and let the dual visions wash over me.

On one path, I press the button, and my fertilized egg begins to grow, dividing and dividing, still too small to see inside the machine, too small to be anything but a hope and dream bound up in nucleotides.

On the other path, I unplug the machine, wash it out, and put it up on Keith's List for sale. I make a decent chunk of money, 'cause the model my mom handed down to me is pretty high quality, even though it's old and been gathering dust in her garage for years.

Back on the first path, I get increasingly excited about the growing fetus as I watch it through the scanner on the womb as months pass. I also get increasingly scared. It's a lot of feelings to have.

Simultaneously, I see myself take the money from selling the womb and fit out my basement music studio with better equipment. I get to work on writing an album for real. Finally.

But in the future where I keep the womb, I don't have to work on writing an album—songs simply pour out of my fingertips, every time I touch my guitar. Songs of fear and worry. Songs of concern and overwhelm. They're beautiful, but haunting. And then the baby comes, born from the machine, and for a time, I stop writing music at all.

For a long time—well, it feels like a long time in the visions, outside in the real world, all of this takes place in the blink of an eye, a mere handful of heartbeats—I watch myself grow into my role as a serious musician and also, but separately, a devoted parent.

The two lives run parallel, centering the same person—me —but become so different in their basic fabrics that those two versions of me grow into entirely different people.

Usually I watch a vision just long enough to decide. It doesn't take long to see which breakfast cereal will make you happier. But this choice is harder, and I watch the two paths for as long as they go.

Then I open my eyes.

I think about what I saw.

Both lives will have their ups and downs. Both lives are filled with music; that's too much a part of me to ever be drowned out.

Only one of the lives holds my child—a perfect, wonderful being so magical that I can't imagine robbing the world of their presence. They are the shape of my heart. The soul of my life. My purpose and my deepest love.

And I know what I have to do.

You won't like this. You may not even believe it.

But I unplug the machine.

Because I can't do that to myself. I don't want to feel that much. I don't want to be overwhelmed and consumed. Eclipsed. I just want to go about my days, writing my music and worrying over trivial decisions about breakfast cereal. That's enough.

Maybe later I'll call my mom, tell her about my decision and describe the amazing grandchild I'm denying her. She'll get a real kick out of that. Then maybe she'll help me pick out the best ways to spend the money I'm about to make from selling the womb. She's really sharp about getting good deals when upgrading studio equipment.

For now, though, I'm going to have a bowl of cereal, poured out of whichever box is still out on the counter. I don't even care what kind it is. I've made enough decisions for today.

Sometimes, two roads diverge in a wood, and you choose to walk down the easier one, even if it means skipping out on an amazing view of the sunset. And that's okay.

24

WHERE HAVE ALL THE MOUSIES GONE

Does it matter what your last thoughts are when you die? If you could choose them—they would be hope, wouldn't they? A bright future. Waiting. Ready. And you're going to miss it, but wouldn't you rather die looking out on a shining expanse of golden sunlight, reflecting off ocean waves and filtering through leafy forests? Cities full of smiling people, whiskers turned up in happiness. Bare paws dancing on the concrete streets, and long tails tied together, turned like skipping ropes as adults, filled with laughter, act like mere kits.

Voices rising together in song, drowning out the whistling breeze but also joining with it, becoming part of the natural world again.

My grandmother died ten years ago when the cats invaded our world, landing their flying saucers on top of our cities, crushing our skyscrapers, and then chasing our people like we were nothing more than animated rag dolls. Entertainment to be toyed with, played with, and maybe eaten. Or maybe left to decay—bones and rotting meat, not good enough even to fill a cat's belly.

We thought they'd never leave. We thought we could never make them.

She was already an old mouse. I take comfort from that. But she died from a broken heart. We lived in a small enough town that the flying saucers didn't land here. We heard the news, reading it every morning, hearing it every afternoon over the airwaves. All the mice who died. All the mice who suffered. The cats' were decades ahead of us in technology, that was clear from their flying saucers alone. What chance did we have?

I think my grandmother could have lived longer if they hadn't come. I don't know. Maybe not much longer. But from the way she wrung her tail in her paws as she writhed on her deathbed, how low her round ears flattened against her head, and the furious speed of her twitching nose during her death throes—I know. It was the despair, the terror, and the heart-breaking disappointment of what was happening to our world —what our peaceful, hopeful civilization had become—that pushed her over.

I stayed beside her, put my paw on her shoulder, whis-pering to her all night long through her fevered nightmares, promising her that we'd defeat the cats. When that didn't work —didn't give her the peace she needed to relax, let go, and die —I switched to lies. I told her the cats had never come. They were only figments in her nightmares—gold and green eyes, gleaming and glaring, scheming and planning, sizing us up and finding us too small to care about. They weren't real. Never had been.

Finally, my words sank through her addled dementia. She found peace. Or maybe that's just a lie I tell myself. Either way, she slept, and she stayed asleep until she was gone.

The lies I told her haunted me for years as I fought in the rebellion, striving to keep the promises I'd made before resorting to lies.

Lies felt like they swirled around me. Lies about how we

were better off with the cats ruling us—keeping our population under control. Lies about how they didn't eat our babies as delicacies, storing them in cages until they were ready to be cooked. Lies about how the advances in technology they brought to us were a fair trade for the lives they took.

And yet, here I am in a rooftop garden, on a rebuilt skyscraper, ready to place a neural helmet, adapted from their technologies on my own head. I see the mice around me, uncertain and scared, barely believing that the cats are finally gone, let alone that we've found a way to use the particle blasters they used against us—reversing the effects—to call back the ghosts of our lost loved ones from the years of war.

We can't really bring them back. Not corporeally. Not permanently. But as I place the helmet on my head, I hear a hum, feel a buzz, and from my memories, it recognizes my grandmother, and the reversed particle blaster draws the final moments of my grandmother's life back, gathering up the particles that gave her consciousness from wherever they've wandered over the years, and casting them into a wispy form in front of me.

I reach out, wishing I could touch her, hold her wrinkled paw. Lay my own paw against the white fur on her muzzle, white with age. Her fur was a glossy chestnut brown in pictures I've seen from before I was born. I never knew her that way.

"Grandma?" I say to the ghost in front of me, summoned by science, held together for these few moments by my need and hope.

She looks at the sky, but then she hears me. Recognition sparks in her eyes. "The saucers..." she begins to ask.

"They're gone, Grandma," I say. "It's been years, but we fought. And we organized. And we fought. And we won."

"The cats are gone?" she asks. If she were corporeal, tears would wet her fur. Instead, her eyes sparkle with emotion— sadness, happiness, I don't know. Just so much emotion. And there isn't time for her to share it. There are only moments left. I know. I've seen others summon the ghosts of their loved ones. They never last long.

And I didn't bring my grandmother here for her to speak to me. I brought her here to let her see. Let her hear me tell the truth this time.

"There's a lot to rebuild," I say, "but yes, we beat them. They're gone."

Grandma smiles, hearing the honesty in my voice, and then begins to fade. Her white face grows paler, translucent, gone.

The particles dissipate, leaving nothing but the view of the city spread out around the rooftop garden and the memories of her in my own mind.

And a beautiful day in a rooftop garden, song rising from the streets below. And no more lies.

I take off the helmet, pass it to the next mouse waiting to say goodbye to a loved one already gone. And finally, I can move on with my life.

25

———

MEET ARCHIVE

Archive was telling stories at the corner table when Cobalt Starstrong came in. Cobalt looked at the rapt audience, mostly Heffen refugees, and thought about joining them. Archive was a wonderful storyteller, but Cobalt had heard him before. So, he took a seat at the bar.

"Bring me something I haven't tried before."

The bartender gave him a nod.

"But, uh, make sure it's something I can *metabolize*. Non-toxic to humans and all that."

The bartender swished his elephantine snout as if to sweep away the mere *suggestion* of him poisoning a regular patron. Especially one that tipped as well as Cobalt.

The drink was ready in a jiff.

Cobalt was just taking his first sip and grimacing at the strength of the frothy, amber concoction when a woman he'd never seen before at the *All Alien Cafe* walked in the door. She was tall. Too tall, he decided, and something about the way she held herself made him think of a bird.

The woman, like Cobalt had, watched Archive and his audience for a moment, before looking around and heading to the bar. In fact, it looked to Cobalt like she was heading toward him. Cobalt knew he was a good looking guy, so he couldn't blame her, and he was working real hard to come up with a clever opening line when the woman stuck out her hand, awkwardly toward him and said, "I'm Maradia. An engineer. From Wespirtech."

Wespirtech scientists were among the most brilliant in the known universe. They had discovered and translated the language of stars, proving stellar sentience once and for all. They were not, however, known for their social skills.

"Have a seat," Cobalt said. Then, to assure himself of his status, he launched straight into a story about the time he tricked a frezzipod into a challenge of wits over the rights to the best magno-billiards table in the cafe. Very little of it was true.

"So, you come here a lot," Maradia asked when he was done. During the story, she'd ordered herself a soda water, and had been taking small sips, almost as if she were looking for something to do. A way to avoid eye contact or fidgeting with her hands.

"Sure," Cobalt answered. "My cargo runs bring me through Crossroads Station a lot. It's a big import/export hub."

"I meant this bar," Maradia said. "You come to this bar a lot."

"Oh, right," Cobalt said. "Home away from home and all that." He thought a moment and added, "Or home away from ship, in my case." He took a few minutes to brag about the specs of his souped-up cargo hauler. Maradia wasn't interested. Her eyes kept drifting to the corner. And Archive.

Annoyed and at a loss for why his charm wasn't working on this strange bird of a woman (let alone why she'd approached him so brazenly in the first place), Cobalt decided it was time to offload her. "You know," he said, "That guy in the corner—*his name is Archive*—is another regular here. And he can weave a yarn like an Abeliod tafetta-spider. You should really go give him a listen."

Maradia stared at Archive.

"You'd be doing yourself a favor," Cobalt said. What he meant was that she'd be doing *him* a favor. Then, he could get back to... well... sitting at the bar and drinking. But, in peace. Without the pressure of flirting with some woman he wasn't interested in anyway.

"He has an audience a lot?" Maradia asked.

"Sure," Cobalt said. "Every time I see him, he's surrounded like that."

Cobalt turned his bar stool so he could look at Archive too. "The Heffen refugees are particular fans."

A group of the fluffy-furred, dog-faced aliens was still crowded around Archive. In comparison, Archive looked especially striking: his skin was smooth and faintly blue, purple-blue; his four arms were long and slender; his eyes were huge, silvery, and faceted. He looked like a cross between a praying mantis and an old Earth Hindu statue.

"I think they like him," Cobalt said, taking an unusual turn toward the ponderous, "because he's a refugee too. He tells stories about his world... Though, he never knew it."

Maradia looked at Cobalt, and Cobalt assumed the look was a question.

"Archive's a robot," he said. "An android, created by his race to carry all the memories of their world and culture. See, when their star went supernova, they weren't technologically advanced enough to save themselves... But they sent out Archive, like a message in a bottle—an android that looked like them, to preserve their physical form, with a memory full of all their art, and history, and culture... He was activated for the first time by the Expansionist explorers who discovered his escape shuttle."

Suddenly, Cobalt felt awkward telling another man's stories.

"Like I said, you should go listen to him."

He thought that brush off would be enough, but Maradia was looking at him curiously now. "You sound..." she said, "...like you've listened to Archive a lot."

"Everyone who's been here long has."

Maradia looked down at her soda water, and, with a strange tremble in her voice, said, "Can you tell me one of his stories?"

Cobalt wasn't sure why this woman, who was so forward with him, was so strangely tentative about Archive. But he suddenly realized there was more going on here than he'd thought. "Sure," he said.

So, Cobalt told Maradia the story of an ancient king on Archive's world who traded each of his four arms in turn to an animal-god for four different improvements to his kingdom: first, sturdy buildings built from the bones of their planet, then aqueducts, followed by magnificent statues and works of art. Finally, the king asked for the animal-god's own children— tamed and civilized—to serve the king's people.

It was a just-so story—a legend on Archive's world to explain the first great city and the domestication of their work animals. The funny thing was, Maradia seemed to have heard it before. She smiled at all the right places. Except... sometimes a moment too soon.

"Now you tell me a story," Cobalt said. "How about the story of how Maradia had her heart broken by Archive?"

"What?" Maradia said, looking startled.

"Well, the way you're acting... I can tell a jilted lover when I see one."

Maradia laughed. "Apparently you can't. Still... You're right, I guess." She stared at the bubbles in her soda water. "He did break my heart."

Cobalt pushed his drink—a frothy amber refill—towards Maradia again. This time, without looking at him, she took sip. Then a few more. Deeper, longer draughts.

"I told you I'm an engineer," she said. "What I didn't say is that I specialize in robotics." Maradia stared at Archive, gesturing with his elegant, long arms in the corner. He had his Heffen audience spellbound. Maradia too.

"I build a lot of semi-intelligent robots on commission," she said. "Mostly, machines that couldn't pass the sentience test if you gave them a cheat sheet. I design them that way—people don't like it when their appliances apply for independent legal standing, turn around, and sue their owners for committing slavery. So, I give my customers what they want."

Maradia looked at Cobalt now. "On the side, I started building sentient models for myself. The fifth one—R5—was an experiment. Could I build a story-telling robot?"

Cobalt was guessing the answer was yes. He felt his stomach sink. "Archive isn't..." He couldn't finish the thought. He'd spent so many hours listening to Archive's stories. *Everyone here had.*

"I succeeded brilliantly," Maradia said with unvarnished pride. "I could have listened to R5 make up stories for hours..." Here, she stared longingly at Archive. "His stories grew more and more complex. He made up a whole world, and all the stories tied together in a beautiful network of history and culture."

Cobalt couldn't believe it, and couldn't help believing it. He'd been such a dunce. Everyone had. "Archive's been lying to us all this time..."

"No!" Maradia said. "He doesn't lie. He's a storyteller."

"Sounds like lying to me."

"You haven't heard the end yet," Maradia said, anger edging her voice. "Don't judge so quickly."

"You have," Cobalt said. "You won't even talk to him anymore."

Maradia glared at Cobalt, a cold stare that warned him she

was almost done with him. Rather than press his point, Cobalt said, "Tell me the end, then."

Maradia softened and sighed. "Eventually, R5 ran out of space. He'd made a whole *world* in his memory, and I hadn't planned for that when I built his brain. First, he overwrote all but the most minimal short term memory. You may have noticed that he's forgetful?"

Cobalt nodded. He'd seen Archive try to tell the same story three times in the same night. Archive was always congenial when his audience objected though.

"Next," Maradia said, "he started overwriting his *own* long term memories."

"You mean," Cobalt said, "he erased you right out?"

"I *tried* supplementing his brain..." Maradia sounded like she was defending herself. To herself. Or, maybe, to Archive long ago. "Every new piece of memory I gave him... He filled them right up. More stories. New stories. It was never enough, and every day he seemed to remember less... *Less of his own life. Less of me...*"

Maradia tried to take another sip of the drink, only to realize she'd already finished it. She ran her finger along the lip of the glass. "Maybe if I hadn't programmed him to love the stories so much... Above all else."

"Couldn't you reprogram him?" Cobalt asked.

Maradia looked at him blankly, like a woman who'd lost a battle a long time ago. "He'd already passed his sentience test. I couldn't do a thing to him without his permission anymore."

"Right, you mentioned that." Cobalt made a mental note to look up information on the *sentience test* later.

"Finally one morning," Maradia said, "I came in and R5 was gone." She paused, looking shaken at the memory. "He called himself *Archive* and told me the story of how he'd been created to save the memories of his dying world, and then he started off on some parable about cold winters... I couldn't stand it. I couldn't listen to his made up tales anymore. Not when everything that *we'd* shared... Every memory that he had of me, and how I'd built him... All of it. Gone."

Maradia bristled. It looked like she was putting back up a shield that she'd constructed to protect herself from the remembered pain. "He really believes he's Archive now. He's telling the truth, as well as he knows it."

Cobalt and Maradia sat quietly for a while.

Eventually, she said, "I brought him to the Refugee Quarter and got him an easy job. I thought he'd fit in here."

"He does," Cobalt said. He'd seen Archive stocking boxes on the docks. He always looked like he was daydreaming. About his world. But, then, a lot of the aliens in the Refugee Quarter of Crossroads Station looked that way. Even if Archive hadn't originally been one of them... He was now.

Maradia stared at Cobalt levelly. He could tell she was trying to size him up. "I didn't come here to tell you this story," she said. "I wanted to check on him, you know. Make sure he's *okay*."

Cobalt leaned back and said, "When I had my heart broken, do you know what I did?"

Maradia looked impatient. She didn't want advice from a man in a bar, and Cobalt knew that. She wanted to know that her errant, mechanical son was safe.

"I came to Archive, and he told me the story of Madame Juhlika and her three husbands."

Maradia's eyes sparked in recognition and interest. "How she was better off without them?"

"Right. And, when I crashed my cargo-hauler—can you guess?"

"Lortiv and his rolling house...?" Maradia smiled, enjoying the game.

"That's the one."

"I know the moral of that story is how the rolling house

wasn't worth it," Maradia said. "But I always wanted one anyway..." Her smile was sheer happiness, and her sentence swallowed itself up in laughter: "I love the way he tells it!"

Cobalt looked at the roboticist next to him, and then he looked at the blue-armed, insect-eyed alien/android in the corner. "I'm sure he'd tell it for you..."

Cobalt said it gently, but Maradia shook her head vehemently. "No, no. I couldn't stand him not recognizing me. I... This is enough."

Cobalt nodded, and then his brow furrowed. He was remembering something Maradia had said about *cold winters.* "Do you know Archive's story of the Mother Draku?"

Maradia looked confused and said, "Not that I recall... no."

So, Cobalt told the story of a Draku-beast whose mother knitted a winter coat for her bald-skinned son out of her own woolly fur. As winter in the Drakur forest grew colder and colder, the mother Draku used up more and more of her fur. She couldn't bear to hear her son crying from the cold. The coats grew larger and woollier, and the mother grew smaller and smaller. When, finally, the son was coiffed in so many thick layers of woolly jackets that he pronounced himself warm, he found that his mother had spun away so much of her fur that nothing was left but her tiny, beating heart. The son swallowed her heart saying, "I will keep your heart with my heart, where neither of our hearts will ever be cold again."

When Cobalt finished the story, Maradia was crying. "That's the parable he tried to tell me... It's about me, isn't it?"

"I think, it's *for* you," Cobalt said.

Maradia stared at Archive through her tears, and the bared feelings on her face were too complex for Cobalt to follow. Finally, though, she looked relieved. Archive may have forgotten the events and facts of his life with her, but his memory of her lived on. In a story.

"Maybe," she said, "I will go listen to him. For a while."

ABOUT THE AUTHOR

Mary E. Lowd is a prolific science-fiction and furry writer in Oregon. She's had more than 200 short stories and a dozen novels published, always with more on the way. Her work has won three Ursa Major Awards, ten Leo Literary Awards, and four Cóyotl Awards. She edited FurPlanet's ROAR anthology series for five years, and she is now the editor and founder of the furry e-zine *Zooscape*. She lives in a crashed spaceship, disguised as a house and hidden behind a rose garden, with an extensive menagerie of animals, some real and some imaginary.

For more information:
marylowd.com

To read Mary's short stories:
deepskyanchor.com

ALSO BY MARY E. LOWD

Otters in Space

Otters In Space

Otters In Space 2: Jupiter, Deadly

Otters In Space 3: Octopus Ascending

Otters In Space 4: First Moustronaut

The Celestial Fragments (A Labyrinth of Souls Trilogy)

The Snake's Song

The Bee's Waltz

The Otter's Wings

The Entangled Universe

Entanglement Bound

The Entropy Fountain

Starwhal in Flight

Xeno-Spectre

Hell Moon

The Ancient Egg

In a Dog's World

Jove Deadly's Lunar Detective Agency

The Necromouser and Other Magical Cats

You're Cordially Invited to Crossroads Station

Queen Hazel and Beloved Beverly

Tri-Galactic Trek

Nexus Nine

Some Words Burn Brightly: An Illuminated Collection of Poetry

Welcome to Wespirtech

Beyond Wespirtech